LAST CHANCE LASSITER

Paul Levine

ISBN: 1494887320
ISBN 13: 9781494887322

For Marcia

At long last, love.

AUTHOR'S NOTE

Here's an e-mail I recently received from a reader: "In your early books, before Jake Lassiter became a sole practitioner, he worked in a large law firm and didn't fit in. But you never tell us the circumstances of his leaving. Was he fired? Did he quit? What was he like as a young lawyer?"

"Last Chance Lassiter" – consider it a prequel to "To Speak for the Dead" – will answer those questions. The broad strokes of Jake Lassiter's backstory are well known to long-time readers. A second-string linebacker with the Miami Dolphins, Jake attended night law school and passed the Florida Bar exam on his fourth try. (He figured it was a computer glitch...the passing, not the failing).

His first job was with the Public Defender's Office, where he learned that most of his clients were guilty, "not always with what they were charged, but damn few were in the running for the Nobel Peace Prize." That led to an offer from a downtown deep-carpet law firm, "because I could try murder cases without peeing my pants."

It's that early time readers wonder about. Just how did the iconoclastic tough guy fit in with those corporate noodle necks? Raymond Chandler's line from "Farewell, My Lovely" comes to mind. "He was about as inconspicuous as a tarantula on a slice of angel food."

What led to Jake leaving the big firm and going out on his own, 235 pounds of solid oak trial lawyer, if you forget about two bad knees and a torn rotator cuff?

"Last Chance Lassiter" takes us from Jake's last day in the big firm to his first case as a two-fisted solo practitioner, a knight in dinged armor driving an ancient Olds 442 convertible – 390 horsepower Rocket V8 – in place of a mighty steed.

So settle back. It's a loud and bumpy ride!

Then, free bonus material. The short story, "Solomon & Lord Sink or Swim" features squabbling lawyers Steve Solomon and Victoria Lord. The sharpest lawyer to barely graduate from Key West School of Law, Solomon is a beer and burger guy. Fresh from Yale, Lord is a Chardonnay and paté gal. The arguers extraordinaire can't agree on "good morning," but somehow they're a winning team in court.

I hope you enjoy both the Lassiter novella and the Solomon & Lord short story.

Paul Levine
Miami
January 2, 2014

"The law is some tricky shit, isn't it?"
—Geena Davis in *"Thelma and Louise"*

ONE

Unnecessary Roughness

The view from the 53rd floor of Southeast Financial Center took in the sparkling turquoise water of Biscayne Bay, the shimmering alabaster buildings of Miami Beach...and black-as-death vultures, which glided in the updrafts just outside my floor-to-ceiling windows.

A man with a literary bent might find some clever symbolism in vultures hovering outside a law office. Carnivores inside and out, that sort of thing. But I am not a man given to symbolism or poetry or allegory. I am an ex-linebacker, an ex-public defender, ex-a-lot-of-things, trying to make an honest day's pay in the greedy and sleazy world of big-time lawyering.

My name is Jake Lassiter.

I was standing at my office window, watching the ugly birds as the drawbridge cranked skyward on the MacArthur Causeway, making several hundred commuters late for work, so that one rich dude could sail north along the shoreline without the inconvenience of a detour into open ocean waters. Maybe there was some symbolism in that, too. Who knows? They don't pay me to plumb deep thoughts. Me, I'm just paid to win.

Back to that Causeway. Years later, the city padres would stop dipping into the till long enough to re-construct the damn thing and eliminate the drawbridge, but this was in my early years as a lawyer. In those days, we still had Eastern Air Lines, The Miami News, and a few words of English were still spoken on Flagler Street downtown. *Eso ya no existe, mi amigo.*

"You set the firm record," said a female voice behind me.

"Yardage in a touch football game?" I replied.

"Billable hours!" It was Cecilia (Cece) Santiago, my secretary, as we still called them in those days. She had not yet become an "assistant," and I had not yet seen my first gray hair. "Lowest ever recorded in firm history. All the other associates are talking about it."

"Those weenies lie on their time sheets. I don't."

"Jerry Pillstein is betting you'll be fired."

"The worm who billed 27 hours in one day?"

"He flew from Miami to L.A., picked up three hours on the time change and worked round the clock."

"Bullshit."

"Mr. Krippendorf gave him a plaque."

"If I wanted a plaque, I'd join the Kiwanis."

"Mr. K told you the firm motto, right?"

I remembered my interview with Lyle Krippendorf, senior partner of the firm. A short, rotund sausage of a man jammed into a silk Italian suit.

"In the law, we eat what we kill," Krippendorf had said, stuffing his face with bloody tenderloin smeared in bearnaise. "You gotta bill 250 hours a month, minimum, or you go on probation, kid."

I'd wanted to give him a forearm shiver, but I needed the work and took the job.

Billing my time. Documenting every breath I took. Leasing out my life by the quarter hour.

■ ■ ■

A few minutes after Cece breezed out of my office, I was sitting at my desk, thumbing through the files I'd been assigned. There was the fashion model, thin as a Q-Tip, who wanted me to sue Starbucks for "poisoning" her Frappuccino by using whole milk instead of skim. There was a nasty divorce where the wife, our client, had scissored off the left sleeve of every one of her husband's sixty-eight custom-made suits and sports jackets. And there was a guy who couldn't believe the City of Coral Gables wouldn't let him keep his 18-foot long Burmese python in the backyard, after it swallowed whole the neighbor's French poodle.

Three yawners. "Boring" was not a boring enough word to convey my lack of emotional involvement in my cases. So what did I want? What would rev my motor?

A cause that's just, a client I like, and a check that didn't bounce. In my short time as a lawyer, I'd seldom found all three in the same case.

My door flew open and Kim Coates, an attorney-in-a-hurry, rushed inside. She shot an unappreciative gaze at my Road Runner and Wile E. Coyote posters, which along with photos of sharks and sports memorabilia, completed my interior decorating.

"Lunch?" she asked, as if forming an entire sentence would take her away from billing enormous amounts of time at outrageous hourly rates. Kim was 32 years old, a tidy brunette with an upturned nose and torso by Jane Fonda. Technically, she was senior to me in the firm by a couple years, which might explain why she insisted on the top position during the hot and sweaty nights we spent together at my place or hers.

"Sure thing." I regretted the extra syllable as a waste of her time.

"Where?"

"Versailles for Cuban sandwiches."

"Strolling guitarists freak me out," she said, "and it's too noisy to work."

"Work? I thought we were eating."

"Mr. K wants us to discuss the credit card class action litigation. We can each bill 90 minutes, including travel time, if we talk business in the car."

3

"Joe's Stone Crab," I suggested.

"Only if we can run the cost through to the client."

"Maybe we should forget lunch and plan a leisurely dinner."

"I'm working late. How about takeout Thai?"

"Your place or mine?"

"The car."

"Romantic."

"Sorry, Jake. I've got an 8 a.m. depo in Palm Beach and need my sleep."

I considered whether to complain about our not spending enough time together, but it seemed too wimpy. We'd been sleeping together – though not often – whenever Kim could find a time slot not required for a hearing, depo, or Pilates class.

Every relationship is a competition between personal autonomy and inter-connectedness. Historically, it's the guy who refuses to compromise, to give up his solitude, or man cave, or drinking buddies. But times have changed. Hard-charging career women like Kim Coates are frequently unwilling to cut back work time for the sweet promise of companionship, cuddling, and multiple orgasms.

A *knock-knock* sounded on the open door, as Cece poked her head into the office. "No lunch for you, *jefe*. Mr. K. has a new client for you to interview."

"As long as it's not another divorce."

"Even worse."

"Nothing's worse."

"Divorce plus spousal abuse. Wife got the stuffing beat out of her."

"Tell me I'm repping her."

"No luck, *jefe*. You for the puncher."

Cece was right. This was worse. You can pick your friends. You can pick mangoes from blooming trees. But an associate in a law firm cannot pick his clients.

■ ■ ■

James Farrell was thirty-five and tennis fit. He wore a tailored tan suit, blue shirt, and yellow tie. His job had something to do with real estate development, but in Miami, that could mean anything from building shopping centers to being a bag man for the zoning department. He seemed to be staring at the leaping marlins on my multi-colored Hawaiian shirt. Maybe a dark suit would instill more confidence, but I always thought the charcoal gray look made lawyers seem like undertakers. I kept a couple ties and a white shirt hanging behind my office door for trips to the courthouse. Otherwise, I was a habitual offender, daily violating the Krippendorf and Associates dress code. Just as I violated the "Wall Decoration Decree," proclaiming that the art committee must approve everything posted on law firm property. I'd already received a stern memo warning me to take down the bloody photos of sharks feeding, as inappropriately suggestive.

I didn't nail my law school diploma to Lyle Krippendorf's textured walls. There were no honors attached to my University of Miami parchment, and it took me an extra year to get though the night division, where I graduated in what I like to call the top half of the bottom third of my class. The diploma covers a crack in the plaster above a toilet at home and forces me to contemplate the divide between law and justice several times each day.

My framed cartoon character posters – Road Runner, Wile E. Coyote, Pepe le Pew, Bugs Bunny – turned Krippendorf's cheeks scarlet whenever he strolled into my office. His eyes would keep flicking toward the walls while he warned me to keep my hours up and reminded me about the next game in the Lawyer's Flag Football League. On those occasions, it was impossible not to believe that I'd been hired for my ability on the football field as much as for my legal acumen.

I said hello to my new client and we shook hands, the guy trying to impress me with his grip. I've had several fingers broken in my playing days, including once when my knuckles got stuck inside a quarterback's face mask. To be honest, I had jammed my hand through the mask in a fruitless effort to either remove the QB's head from his shoulders, or failing that, to gouge out his eyes. Yeah, I got penalized for unnecessary roughness, surely a non-sequitur where football is concerned.

So, Farrell's grip didn't bother me, though my knuckles *crickety-cracked* with the sound of a bowling ball scattering pins.

"You gonna keep that bitch from getting my money?" Farrell started out.

"Let's talk about the criminal case first."

"Domestic battery and spousal abuse. It's bullshit."

I thumbed through the skinny file on my desk. "Your wife went to the E.R. with lacerations and contusions"

"She slipped and fell in the bathroom."

I flipped another page. "Third trip to the hospital. So many clumsy wives these days."

"I got a doctor who'll swear the bruises came from falling on the tile floor."

"But is it true?"

"Does it matter?"

"To me, it does."

The woman who raised me, Granny Lassiter, told me that only gutter snipes and trailer park lowlifes hit their women. "A Lassiter man, no matter how drunk or angry, never lays a hand on a woman that don't want to be touched."

Farrell gave me a long, hard look. "It just occurred to me. Jake Lassiter, right?"

"Yeah."

He shot a look toward the credenza where an autographed football bore Coach Shula's signature. He had written something about admiring my "pluck." Good word when adjectives like "athletic" and "skillful" would be blatant exaggerations.

"You used to play for the Dolphins," Farrell said.

"Not very long and not very well, but yeah."

"You're 'Wrong Way Lassiter!'"

Oh, shit. That again.

"I was there the day you scored a touchdown for the wrong team."

"Scored a safety," I corrected him.

"Right. And the Dolphins lost by a point to the Jets. Am I right?"

Yeah, the bastard was right. My playing time came on the suicide squad, the kickoff team. At the start of the second half of that long-ago game, I collided head-on with the returner. The ball popped out, I scooped it up, got turned around, and carried the ball into the wrong end zone where I triumphantly hurled it into the stands. A grinning monkey of a man humiliating himself in front of a national television audience.

I could blame the snow and fog at the old Shea Stadium. I could blame the concussion I suffered on the tackle. But lately, I've just taken personal responsibility, which is more than my clients ever do. I played as hard as I could, made two decent plays – the jarring tackle, the fumble recovery – then screwed up. Still, there is one gnawing fact that has eaten away at me all these years.

"Thing is," I said to Farrell, "the replay showed my knee was down by contact when I recovered the ball. The play should have been blown dead. Our ball. We win by a point instead of losing by one."

"A bad ruling." He gave me a sly little grin, then stood up and paced around my office. "I can relate."

"How's that?"

"Life's not fair. You make one boneheaded play in your career, that's all anybody remembers. Same thing with my deal if I get convicted of this bullshit. Basically, I'm a good guy."

"A prince," I said, agreeably.

He spent a moment admiring my rack of baseball bats, then pulled one from its slot. The bat was a gift from a client in lieu of a fee. The client, a sports memorabilia dealer, claimed the bat was used by Edgar Renteria of the Marlins to drive in the winning run in the seventh game of the 1997 World Series. Indeed, Renteria's signature appeared on the bat. But I sensed neither the signature nor the provenance was real. My client, after all, made most of his money engaged in what the federal government considers mail fraud.

Clients are like that. If they'll cheat their customers, they're just as likely to lie to their lawyers.

"You don't want to see me take a fall because of one slip-up," Farrell continued.

"Except in my case, the ref blew the call. In your case, the drift I'm getting is that you beat up your wife."

He took a practice swing with the bat. "I'll swear under oath that I never touched her."

"In my experience, honest people don't need to put their hand on a Bible to tell the truth, and with dishonest people, it makes no difference." I slipped Farrell's booking photo out of the file. "When you were arrested, your face had fingernail scratches, and the knuckles of your right hand were raw."

"Whose side are you on, Lassiter? I told you I got a doctor who'll back me up."

"I know doctors who'll swear a paraplegic can win the decathlon."

"So what's your strategy? What's your legal advice?"

"Plead guilty to a lesser offense. Simple assault, maybe. Get probation and some counseling."

"And give that bitch ammo for the divorce? Fuck that."

I didn't like Farrell the moment I saw him, and my opinion hadn't changed for the better. I glanced out the windows. Three black vultures were parasailing in the updrafts. Just floating there without any apparent effort. Lucky birds.

"What is it you're not telling me, Farrell?"

Another practice swing. Strike two. "You're so smart, you figure it out."

It only took a second. "You can't plead because you're got a prior. No probation for you."

He shrugged. "Ex-girlfriend claimed I beat her up. I never should have pleaded to that one."

Damn clients. Always keeping secrets. "Guys who hit women," I told him, "they're scum-sucking bottom feeders."

"Watch it, pal."

"They've got doubts about who they are, what they're made of."

"I don't care if you're a former jock. I know karate."

"That what you used on your wife?"

"Warning you, Lassiter."

"Those doubts, I mentioned. It's about their manhood."

"You calling me a...?"

"Got nothing to do with your sexual leanings. But you know what you are? A coward. A pussy who pretends to be a tiger."

That did it. He leapt from his chair and herky-jerked around my desk. I got to my feet and he stopped, the baseball bat in his right hand. If he swung at my head, I'd duck and plow a right hook into his gut. Once he threw up on my desk, I'd rub his face in it.

He cocked the bat, waggled it back and forth.

"Face it Farrell, you don't have the balls to do it."

Just then, the son-of-a-bitch uncorked a swing, aimed at my head.

TWO

More Bang for the Yen

I didn't know this until it was too late, but at precisely the moment James Farrell swung the baseball bat at my head, Lyle Krippendorf was strolling down the corridor outside my office with two potential clients and my alleged girlfriend Kim Coates. Krippendorf must have heard raised voices – mine and Farrell's – from the other side of the door and quickly decided not to include my office as a stop on the tour.

I can't blame him. Why risk introducing your loose cannon associate to a couple of middle-aged, three-piece suited Japanese bankers who could be worth a fortune in fees, once they stopped bowing and smiling? At least, Kim Coates could be depended on to say and do the right thing.

Afterwards, I imagined what Krippendorf would have told them: "Ms Coates is one of our outstanding associates. She'll show you our state-of-the-art library. One hundred percent digital, and you folks sure know all about that."

At about that moment, Krippendorf would have heard a thud shake the door to my office.

Inside, I was trying to fend off a client with rage issues who was swinging my baseball bat. I raised my arms to protect my head, and the bat glanced off my left forearm. The guy swung more like Edgar Allan Poe than Edgar Renteria.

I fired a short right hand into his gut and he *whoomped* and staggered backwards but didn't puke. He also didn't drop the bat. He swung again, one-handed, this time aiming at my knees. I side-stepped, but he clipped me on the hip. I winced. The sting reminded me of a hip pointer I suffered in a pileup on the frozen tundra of Lambeau Field. The swing left Farrell off balance. I grabbed his shirt collar with one mitt and slung him into the door with a loud thwomp.

"How's it feel to get pushed around, tough guy?" I taunted him.

Now, with both hands on his shirt collar, I slammed him into the door again.

Thwomp.

"Got some idea how your wife felt or do you need some more?"

He gasped but still had enough air to yell at me. "You second string loser! I'll get you disbarred."

That deserved another, so I slammed him into the door yet again.

Twice. *Thwomp. Thwomp.*

The door banged open and Farrell flew out, barreling into the corridor toward Krippendorf, whose back was turned as he spoke to the potential clients from Tokyo. "With my firm, Shimono Bank will get more bang for its yen."

Farrell bounced off Krippendorf and crumpled to the floor. Krippendorf staggered but didn't fall. The fat fart had a low center of gravity. Without seeming perturbed, he launched into damage control, bowing to his visitors: *"Taihen moushi wake arimasen."*

The Japanese men just bowed and smiled back.

"Just what kind of insane asylum are you running here, Krippendorf?" Farrell demanded from his position on the floor.

"I'm sorry, Mr. Farrell," Krippendorf said. "Jake, apologize to your client."

"He's not my client."

"Regardless, apologize!"

"I'm sorry. I made a mistake."

"That's a start. Go on."

"No, Krip, I'm apologizing to you. I'm sorry I took your job offer and deprived you of another ass-smooching sycophant. I don't belong here. No one with self-respect does."

Krippendorf just stood there, mouth agape, as I headed down the corridor and toward a new life.

THREE

Flirting with Disbarment

"Take a memo," I said.

"To whom?" Cece asked.

"To me."

"You want to remind yourself to give me a raise?"

We were in my new office. My oceanfront office, in the loosest sense of the word. I was in a ground floor windowless hovel of a room in a parking garage, located in an alley just off Lincoln Road on Miami Beach. If you were on the roof of the garage and climbed the ladder up the exterior of the elevator shaft, then stretched on tippy-toes, and were six-feet-two to start with, you could see a slice of the Atlantic Ocean. Unfortunately, from inside the bowels of the garage, I could see only the four concrete walls of my twelve by twelve compartment.

Prisoners on death row have better accommodations.

On the other hand, there was plenty of parking, and the building wouldn't blow down in a hurricane.

"I will live by no code but my own," I recited to Cece.

"Huh?"

"Write it down. Type it up. That's my mantra from now on."

"You will live by no code but your own?"

"You got it."

"What about the Florida statutes? The U.S. Constitution?"

"Mere suggestions. I'm tired of selling out. Tired of playing by the other guys' rules. Guys like Krippendorf."

"Okay, okay." She scribbled something on her notepad. Hopefully, it was a close facsimile to what I had dictated.

"Next. My word is my bond."

"Nice one," she agreed.

"From anyone else, I want an affidavit. Write it down."

Cece scribbled on her pad. "How 'bout a mantra about not hitting people?"

I shook my head. "Gotta be a promise I can keep."

"Anything else?"

I thought a moment before speaking. It's not something I always do. "I will treat judges with respect and dignity..."

"For a change," she said.

"Unless they're fools or crooks," I added.

Again, Cece took notes, then wrinkled her forehead. "What good is your code without customers?"

"Clients, Cece. We call them clients."

I didn't hear the knock on the door at first. One concussion too many may have affected my hearing. But Cece turned her head that way, and then I heard a pounding that competed with the sounds of tires squealing on the nearby up-ramp.

"Come in!" I shouted.

The door opened and a stocky man in his forties wearing a grey suit stepped in and looked around dubiously. "This a law office?"

"Close the door," I told him. "Those car fumes are wicked."

He did as he was told. "Are you Jake Lassiter?"

"Yes, if you're a new client. No, if you're a process server."

"George Grumley," he introduced himself. "The Florida Bar."

Cece gave me an *oh-shit* look and left the office.

Grumley walked toward my desk and handed me a business card. I read aloud: "Chief Investigator, Eleventh Circuit."

For a moment, I wondered if I might have forgotten to pay my dues.

"Your client James Farrell filed a complaint," chief investigator Grumley said. "Claims you attacked him, and he's got the medical bills to prove it."

"He came at me with a baseball bat."

"That so?"

"I was defending myself. Under the stand-your-ground law, I could have shot him with a machine gun."

"Not the way he tells it."

"So he's a liar and a wife beater."

"Wife beater? You're not disclosing an attorney-client communication, are you, Mr. Lassiter?"

Damn.

"Because frankly, I've seen your file, and for someone who's practiced as short a time as you have, you certainly have been flirting with disbarment."

Disbarment.

To a lawyer, it's a word with the emotional heft of say, cancer. Inoperable, terminal, stage four cancer.

"Look, Mr. Grumley. I might have called Farrell a few names and insulted his manhood. But he was the aggressor."

"Are you familiar with Bar Rule seven-D, Mr. Lassiter?"

"Not really, but if it's only number seven, how important can it be?"

"'Lawyers must comport themselves with...'" He shot a look toward the corner of the room where the Wile E. Coyote and Road Runner posters sat on the floor, waiting to be hung. "Dignity."

"Sounds like a slap-on-the-wrist offense. Can I plead *nolo* and get a sternly worded letter from Tallahassee?"

"Assault and battery is a felony, and a felony is a disbarable offense."

"'Disbarable?' Is that even a word?"

"Your flippancy will be noted."

"Now 'flippancy' is definitely a word. But a funny one. No way can you say 'flippancy' and not smile."

Without warning, Grumley snatched a piece of paper from my desk. And the guy didn't even have a warrant. Reading aloud he said, "'I will live by no code but my own.'"

"So?"

"Did you write that?"

"What is this, the Spanish Inquisition? You punish a man for his thoughts?"

Grumley backed toward the door, still holding my sheet of notepaper. "Don't bother unpacking, Mr. Lassiter. I'm very good at my job, and I'm making it my business to pull your ticket."

FOUR

The Goodbye Girl

"**Y**ou really piss me off," Kim Coates said.

"I wasn't looking at that topless girl," I defended myself.

"I don't care who you look at."

"Lots of freckles...everywhere."

"Forget the girl. I'm talking about you! Your career, or what's left of it."

We were walking on the Tenth Street Beach, where young men and young women – okay, male and female models from the local agencies – were playing volleyball. Others sunbathed, some of the females without their tops.

I hadn't seen Kim since I was either fired or quit, depending who was telling the story.

"I can't believe you dissed Krippendorf in front of important new clients," Kim went on. "He can keep you from getting a job in this town."

"Don't want a job. I'm flying solo. Or duo."

"What does that mean?"

"Why don't you quit Krippendorf? Come work with me."

"Are you crazy? I'm on partnership track."

"You want to be Krippendorf's partner? Snakes have warmer blood."

"Jake, do you even know what it takes to be a successful lawyer?"

17

"The morals of a pickpocket?"

I heard Kim sigh as we passed a volleyball court where two female models were arguing whether a spiked ball was in or out. "Your eye lift make you blind?" one goaded the other.

My plan was to jog north 30 blocks or so to the Fontainebleau Hotel, then turn around and head back. But Kim didn't seem to want to run. Or talk.

Having picked some juries, I consider myself an authority on body language. At the very least, I know that a juror who coils up like a cobra when I'm asking questions is not likely to be my champion behind closed doors. Just now, Kim had folded her arms across her chest and was walking three yards in front of me. Maybe a fullback dive could close the distance, but a quarterback sneak surely would not.

I decided to change the subject just a bit, maybe strike some common ground. I liked Kim. I wasn't entirely sure what I was getting from the relationship, but she was smart and sexy, and after a half pitcher of margaritas, she was known to shed her clothes like a snake molting.

"You know what I hate about our profession?" I asked.

"Success?"

"Perception. How clients perceive us. There I was, meeting with Farrell, and he just assumed I'd go along with his lying under oath."

"So?"

"It's insulting!"

"Wake up, Jake. If people didn't lie, cheat, and steal, they wouldn't need you. Jesus, sometimes you're so..."

"Idealistic?"

"Naive."

We passed another beach volleyball game, one of the female models loudly threatening to sue another for aiming a spike at her surgically perfected nose.

"When we first met," Kim said, "you seemed so together. So manly. I thought you were partnership material."

"Not if I have to be judged by someone else's standards."

"Then you sailed off course."

"Sailed my course."

"Standing up for that senile old medical examiner."

"Doc Riggs isn't senile."

"He forgot who he was working for and got fired for helping defense lawyers."

"For telling the truth!"

"He went off the reservation."

"Why? Because he wouldn't fudge an autopsy for the state attorney? Jeez, the medical examiner is supposed to be neutral, not an arm of the state. They already have enough arms."

"Like I said, Jake. Naive."

We trundled through the sand, passing sunbathers spread-eagled on their beach towels, as motionless as if shot by snipers from passing cruise ships. The scent of coconut oil was in the air. From a café across the street, I heard a band playing funky Afro-Caribbean music.

"So, we're still okay, right?" I didn't like the lameness in my voice. Whatever happened to Big Bad Jake Lassiter, wooer of groupies in every city in the Eastern Conference, even Buffalo.

Kim exhaled another sigh, turned away and said, "Good luck, Jake."

"Good luck?"

"With your practice. And your life."

She walked away, kicking up sand in her wake.

FIVE

A Midget Walks into a Bar

"**S**he dumped you?" Cece sounded bewildered. "That piranha in pantyhose dumped you?"

"Shark," I said. "Kim has a bigger appetite than a piranha."

We were in my garage-office, and my trusty secretary was doing her best to be supportive, not one of her strong suits.

"Are you hurting, *jefe*? Because she's not worth it."

"Thanks, Cece."

"Not that you're such a bargain."

"Thanks, again."

"You know what you need? Work."

"Great. But I don't have any clients."

"Sure you do. They answered your ad in the Beach Gazette."

"What ad?"

Cece gave me her sly smile and handed me a giveaway tabloid newspaper. Right there on the open page was the silhouette of a man in a suit – me presumably – in a boxing stance. The caption said: "Trial lawyer Jake Lassiter. He'll fight for you."

I didn't believe in lawyers advertising. My mug on the back of a bus or a billboard? No thanks.

I shoved the newspaper to the side. "Aw, Jeez, Cece. That's even below my standards."

"Don't worry about it. Your first customer, excuse me, client, will be here in five minutes."

■■■

"I want you to sue the Biscayne Times over its matchmaking ads," said Myron, a pot-bellied 45-year-old with a slipping toupee.

"You didn't meet the love of your life? I'm shocked."

"It's not just that."

"There are no guarantees. I'm pretty sure there's a disclaimer."

"They're letting the women lie," Myron barreled ahead. "'Supermodel looks.' Then she uses a picture that's gotta be 30 years old. Another one says, 'great sense of humor.' I told her my best midget walks into a bar joke, and she didn't laugh. Then there's the one who claimed her body type was 'athletic and toned.' The woman was a blimp."

"So you want me to..."

"Sue the Times for allowing false advertising."

I watched the guy as he fingered the fringes of his toupee. There was a gravy stain on his white guayaberra just above a missing button about nipple high. He reeked of cigarette smoke, and I'd guess his age at north of fifty.

"What about your ad, Myron? What'd you say about yourself?"

"How's that relevant?"

"Oh, trust me on this."

"My ad said something like, 'Fit, handsome, charming ex-tennis champion, 39, seeks smart, sexy woman 18 to 29.'"

"Tennis champ?" I just wanted to know if there was one true statement in his profile.

"Table tennis, actually. Third place in summer camp back in the day."

"May I be blunt, Myron?"

"Sure..."

"Get the hell out of my office."

■■■

21

Potential client number two was a very angry man who wanted to sue his wife for the return of his kidney. Seems he donated the organ to her, and she expressed her gratitude by having an affair with the transplant surgeon.

I put down my legal pad and wondered if I had chosen the wrong career. I could have coached football at a junior high school somewhere in Colorado. Ski in the winter, hike in the summer. Leave the bizarro craziness of Miami behind.

■■■

One more customer – I'd started adopting Cece's term – was waiting when the one-kidneyed litigant left. This guy was in his early thirties with his arm in an elevated cast. It didn't take a genius to figure out this was a personal injury case – *ka-ching, ka-ching* – might be in my future.

"So I'm the passenger in this taxi..." the guy begins.

Good news. Taxi companies have plenty of insurance.

"And the cabbie slams on the brakes. I mean, slammed them to the floor, and I go flying right into the back of the front seat and break my elbow."

"Sounds like a winner." Finally, I thought. "What's the reason the cabbie hit the brakes so hard?"

The guy suddenly got a sheepish look.

"What?" I asked.

"I hope it doesn't hurt my case, but at the time he hit the brakes, I'd pulled a gun and was robbing him."

■■■

My last potential client of the morning was an African-American woman in her late twenties, wearing a summery sleeveless dress festooned with sunflowers. She said her name was Sherrell Johnson.

"You ever handle copyright infringement cases?" she asked.

"Never."

"Do you know anything about that area of the law?"

"I learned a little in law school, enough to get a C in the course."

She studied me a moment. She seemed to be considering whether it was a waste of time to talk further with such a sorry-ass lawyer. "You ever hear the name Cadillac Johnson?" she asked.

I shook my head. "Nope. Should I?"

"My grandfather. A rock-and-roller back in the fifties. What about M.C. Silky?"

"Sure. Hip-hop D.J. got his start on the Beach. Now he's a big-time rapper. I think I read he's got a movie coming out."

"He's a thief."

"Go on."

"He stole Grandad's song. *I'm Leaving You, Baby.*"

I shrugged. "Never heard of it."

"Silky laid in some rap, calls it *Don't Cry, Baby.*"

"That one, I've heard."

She opened her purse and handed me a compact audio cassette. The cover art showed a bare-chested, heavily muscled multi-tattooed African American man, bursting out of heavy chains. "M.C. Silky Unchained."

"Ms. Johnson..."

"Call me Sherrell."

"Sherrell, I know this much. Recording stars have a big hit, people come out of the woodwork, claiming plagiarism."

She stiffened in her chair. "Grandad didn't come out of the woodwork," she fired back. "He paid his dues. Played juke joints and fish fries and clubs where you could get your throat slashed, and he's got nothing to show for it."

"But is that M.C. Silky's fault?"

"He stole Grandad's song, dammit!"

"Okay. Okay."

"Punk-ass rapper's making millions. Grandad's on food stamps."

Everything about Sherrell Johnson rang true. The love for her grandfather. The indignation that he'd been ripped off. I would need to listen to both songs, then hire an expert witness to dissect them. M.C. Silky would doubtless be represented by deep-carpet lawyers with more resources than I could muster. There'd be lots of discovery, a ton of costs. Not easy for a lawyer flying solo.

"Are you able to pay a retainer?" I asked.

"No way. You have to take the case on a contingency fee."

"If I take the case, and let me emphasize 'If,' I'll fight like hell for you, just like it said in the ad."

"What ad?"

"In the Beach Gazette."

"I didn't see any ad. Who would choose a lawyer that way?"

"You'd be surprised. Or maybe not. How'd you get my name?"

"I was referred by another lawyer. A pretty distinguished one at that."

"Who?"

"Mr. Lyle Krippendorf."

"What?"

"He spoke very highly of you. His exact words were: 'Jake Lassiter's the man to litigate this. He packs a helluva punch.'"

SIX

One Third of Nothing Is Nothing

"Why the hell would Krippendorf send a client your way?" Doc Charlie Riggs asked.

"Because he thinks I'm a good lawyer."

"Hah!" Doc Riggs hacked up a wad of phlegm and spat at the trunk of a cabbage palm tree. Doc was in his sixties, a small, compact man with strong hands from clipping through bones and pulling out intestines hand-over-hand in thousands of autopsies. A bent fish hook held his spectacles together where they'd lost a screw.

We were in the backyard of his house, just off Krome Avenue, so far west as to be nearly in the Everglades. It was an old Cracker house built in the 1930s. Steep metal roof, white painted wood, and a covered wrap-around porch. Wearing work boots, a wide-brimmed straw hat, and faded lab pants, Doc Riggs was spading fertilizer between rows of lemon trees. I was pushing the old geezer's wheelbarrow.

"You got a second reason?" he asked. "Maybe a more logical one than he admires your legal skills."

"Krippendorf represents M.C. Silky's record label. He had to turn down representing Cadillac Johnson because of the conflict of interest, so he told Sherrell to call me."

"So of all the lawyers in Miami, and we're talking thousands now, Krippendorf picks you."

"Yeah."

"As his opponent!"

"You're saying he thinks he can beat me."

"Like a drum."

"Okay, he thinks I'm a screw-up, a loser, a washout."

Doc Riggs examined a leaf on one of the lemon trees. "Jump in anytime, Charlie, and disagree."

"You want my advice, Jake?"

"That's why I'm here."

He shoveled a wad of fertilizer onto the base of a tree trunk. "Turn down the case."

"Too late. I told the client's granddaughter I'd take the case, subject to a music expert supporting the claim of plagiarism."

"You get a deposit for costs?"

"Not a cent."

"A retainer for fees?"

"Nope. A straight contingency. One third of the recovery."

"One third of nothing is nothing."

"Thanks for the vote of confidence."

"Thought you wanted the truth. That's what you always told me."

I positioned myself in the sparse shade of a lemon tree. There was no breeze this far from the ocean, and I had soaked through my orange Hurricanes t-shirt and felt droplets of sweat running down my back into the waistband of my running shorts. "When I was in seventh grade, you came to my civics class down in Key Largo. You remember?"

"Hell no. I talked to a lot of little shits from Key West to Fort Pierce back in those days."

"It was Law Week, or something like that. We were learning about the criminal justice system, and you told us what the medical examiner did."

"Must have grossed you out."

"Not me. I loved it. Anyway, you told the kids. *Jus est ars boni...* something or other."

"*Jus est ars boni et aequi.* Law is the art of the good and the just." Charlie exhaled a sigh. "Don't believe everything carved in marble pediments."

"Hell, I don't. I know justice doesn't just flow from the law like coins from a slot machine. You gotta fight for it. You gotta put everything on the line for it."

Charlie pulled up the brim of his straw hat and squinted at me through his eyeglasses. "You talking about your case or mine?"

"You rolled over, Charlie. You gave up when you wouldn't let me sue the bastards who fired you."

"You're too young. You don't understand."

"I understand you can't fear losing. You can't be afraid of going up against stronger adversaries."

"I knew what I was facing. Powerful people wanted me out of the M.E.'s job. They would find a way to win. They always do."

"They? The big, scary they..."

"The power structure, Jake. In my case, the state attorney, the county mayor, and the sheriff, not to mention their big-money supporters downtown. In your case, should you be foolish enough to take it, you'll be facing a deep carpet lawyer who contributes to every judge's re-election and has wormed his way into the very same group."

"Don't you see it, Charlie? The power structure, whoever the hell they are, can only scare us if we let them. They're just shadows."

"They're real, dammit! That's why I didn't fight them. They would have crushed me, just like they're gonna crush you."

SEVEN

Reversing the Hook

It was a neighborhood of liquor stores, hubcap shops, and crumbling apartment buildings off 27th Avenue, just north of the Miami River. A silver Range Rover with tinted windows rolled by, hip-hop electro sounds of Afrika Bambaataa coming from inside.

I was driving my Olds 442 ragtop with Sherrell Johnson riding shotgun. The vintage car was canary yellow and the huge engine rumbled agreeably.

Ignoring the stares of a half-dozen gangbangers, I parked in front of the Palmetto Arms apartments. I didn't know if the place was named for the tree or the bug, the Florida cockroach. It was three-stories of crumbling concrete-block and stucco. No elevator, so we hauled ass to the third floor, with me hoping that my car would not be taken for a joy ride, stripped, or shipped to Central America by the time we came out.

As we walked along the third floor corridor, Sherrell said, "There's a retirement home we've been looking at down in Kendall. Clean. Quiet. Expensive."

"If we win this case," I said, "money won't be a problem."

I could hear the singing before Sherrell used a key to open the door to number 319.

"I'm leaving you baby...
Got to say goodbye..."

She swung the door open. Inside, sitting at the kitchen table was a lean, white-haired African-American man in his seventies. He played a weathered acoustic guitar and kept singing, ignoring us.

"I'm leaving you baby...
Don't ask why.
I'm leaving you baby...
Baby, baby, baby don't cry."

He put the guitar on the table and looked up at me. "I'm Cadillac Johnson. Thanks to everyone for coming tonight. Stick around for the girls, especially our headliner, Miss Blaze Starr herself."

I was gaping until he broke into a wide grin. "Aw, c'mon, Mr. Lassiter. Just messing with you. I ain't senile."

I let out a breath and smiled. "You have a sweet voice, Mr. Johnson."

"Call me, Cadillac. And how 'bout the words and music? Wrote that back in the summer of '59. Just broke up with this lady." He smiled again. "'Cause I'd met Sherrell's grandmother."

Picking up his guitar, Cadillac finished the song. When he was done, I applauded. He offered me a drink. I declined and took a seat next to him. He appraised me with kind eyes. I didn't see any of the anger his granddaughter seemed to carry around like a sack of heavy rocks.

"Now, listen to this." Sherrell reached into her handbag and pulled out a cassette. A ghetto blaster – a boom box the size of a suitcase – sat on the kitchen table. Sherrell placed the cassette in the slot and hit PLAY. M.C. Silky began singing.

"Don't cry baby...
You're my sexy lady.
Don't cry baby..
Baby, baby, baby."

It was louder than Cadillac's song. A faster beat, too. But I couldn't deny the similarities of melody and lyrics. Was it illegal plagiarism though? I didn't know enough to venture either a musical or a legal opinion.

"Did you hear how Silky reversed Grandad's hook?" Sherrell said.

"Mine's up-down," Cadillac said. <u>Ba</u>-by, <u>ba</u>-by. His is down-up. Ba-<u>by</u>, ba-<u>by</u>.

"I think I heard it. But I can't say for sure. And I've got to warn you. These cases are tough. Unless an expert backs you up, we're—""

"Don't see why," Cadillac interrupted. "If I stole your wallet, I'd go to jail."

"There's sort of a presumption against the people suing bigtime performers. Most recording stars have been sued. Mick Jagger. Michael Bolton, Brian Wilson. And they almost always win."

"Ain't about the money, Mr. Lassiter. "Stealing my song's like taking part of me. You understand that?"

I chewed it over a second. "I think so. Your music is your legacy. It's what you leave behind."

The old man smiled warmly and turned to his granddaughter. "The boy gets it."

Then he started singing softly to himself, and I figured it was time to go.

EIGHT

The Florida Bar vs. Jacob Lassiter

Willard Buckstrom's chambers smelled of dry leather and cigarette smoke.

Even in those days, smoking was not permitted in the old limestone courthouse on Flagler Street. Except in Judge Buckstrom's chambers. His Honor chain-smoked Camels, so he could hardly complain when lawyers lit up.

I don't smoke.

I don't know if James Farrell – my client for ten minutes before I slugged him – had the dirty habit. He didn't try lighting up today, not with his jaw wired shut. I gave him a tight little grin when I walked into chambers and sat across the table from him. His grimace was even tighter.

Next to Farrell was George Grumley, the Florida Bar investigator who didn't like my interior decorating or my attitude. He acknowledged me by a little head shake, left to right and back again, sort of a negative hello.

Judge Buckstrom's job was to hear a bit of evidence and file recommendations with the Bar. That could include everything from dismissing Farrell's complaint against me to a public scolding called a "censure," or even suspension or disbarment. A mahogany plaque for my wall and an "attaboy" were probably out of the question.

"Let's cut to the meat," Judge Buckstrom said, perhaps thinking of the bacon cheeseburger he usually had for lunch. "Mr. Lassiter, what the heck prompted you to strike Mr. Farrell?"

"Because he told me was gonna..."

"Objection, hearsay!" Grumley called out.

"Sustained." The judge flicked his cigarette lighter and put the spark to a Camel.

"Judge, I thought the rules of evidence were relaxed for this sort of hearing," I said.

"They are and they aren't." Really sounding like a judge now.

"Meaning?"

The judge exhaled three smoke rings. "I'll give you some latitude but not a lot of longitude."

Grumley nodded as if this were the wisest statement he'd ever heard. Me? I didn't know what the hell the judge was talking about. His Honor was like that. Trying to sound profound, he was capable of unleashing strings of non sequiturs.

Before ascending to the bench, as they say, as if the judge were a deity, Buckstrom had been a partner in a law firm defending nursing homes that allowed patients to develop bed sores, drown in their own vomit, and in one notable case, get eaten by an alligator. Really. The poor old guy wandered out the front door of the nursing home and fell into a canal bordering the property.

"So not every rule of evidence applies, Your Honor?" I ventured.

"Precisely. But not exactly."

"I see." But of course, I was blind.

"We'll relax some rules without getting all loosey-goosey," the judge said.

This time, I nodded. I might as well pretend to know what was going on.

"So let me ask again," the judge instructed. "Without telling me what Mr. Farrell said to you, why did you strike him?"

I thought about my answer a moment. It was a quiet moment, except for Farrell slurping water through a straw.

"Because based on what he said, which I won't repeat, I knew he was going to—"

"Objection!" Grumley sang out. "Violates attorney-client privilege."

"Sustained." A dry, hacking smoker's cough came from somewhere deep inside the judge who then turned to Farrell. "Do you waive the privilege?"

Through his locked jaw, Farrell murmured, "No *shur.*"

"Should we try again, Mr. Lassiter?"

"I don't know, Your Honor. You're handcuffing me."

"Not yet, Mr. Lassiter. Not yet."

The judge tapped some ashes into a crystal bowl and opened the file. I'm pretty good at reading upside down, a useful skill when visiting opposing lawyers' offices. From what I could see, he was reviewing Grumley's investigative report.

After a moment, the judge read aloud. "'I will live by no code but my own?' What's that mean, Mr. Lassiter?"

"It's just a personal philosophy."

On the other side of the table, Grumley snickered.

"Meaning what? You don't abide by the statutes of the state of Florida?"

"It's always my intent to follow the law, Your Honor."

"But? Do I hear a 'but' coming?"

"But sometimes the law doesn't achieve justice."

"You don't say." The judge's voice was thick with sarcasm. "And here I've been sitting on the bench all these years thinking everything worked perfectly."

"I get your point, judge."

"Do you? There's nothing wrong with the law. The law draws lines. When you cross that line, you create chaos. We depend on the justice system to restore order. Sometimes the system works, and sometimes it doesn't, but not because the law is flawed. It's the humans who run the system who break down."

"All I'm saying judge, sometimes you have to walk pretty close to that line to do justice."

"Like your friend Dr. Charles Riggs did?"

"What's he gotta do with this?"

"I know all about your so-called pro bono work for that old coot."

"He's a good man."

"He tanked a murder case, let a scumbag walk free."

"The prosecutor hid exculpatory evidence from the autopsy. All Doc Riggs did was tell the truth."

The judge *harrumphed*. I'd violated one of the primary rules of the trial lawyer. Never contradict a judge in his own arena. Wearing his robes, the judge is king of his chambers and courtroom. The rest of us are his humble supplicants. Or at least, we're supposed to be.

"So just what entitled you to cross the line and slug your client?"

"That's what I've been trying to tell you, Your Honor. The man wanted to perjure himself and have me help him do it."

"*Thash* a lie!" Farrell said through his locked jaw. Grumley put a calming hand on his wrist.

"Even if it's true," the judge said, "you don't hit the man. You just withdraw from the case."

"He took a swing at me with a baseball bat."

"In your office?"

"I collect bats. "Barry Bonds. Mark McGuire. Sammy Sosa."

"You collect any from guys who didn't break the rules?"

"Edgar Renteria. That's the one Farrell swung at me."

Farrell was shaking his head and saying something that sounded like "No *shit!*"

"I still don't get it, Mr. Lassiter. You say, number one, your client wanted you to use perjured testimony then, number two, he swung a baseball bat at you. What are you leaving out?"

"In between one and two, I called him a liar, a scum-sucking bottom feeder, and a coward."

"Anything else?"

"I think I might have questioned his manhood, too."

The judge clucked his disapproval. "Do you have anger management problems, Mr. Lassiter?"

"Hey, Judge. I'm not the one who swung the bat."

"No, but you're the one who incited the incident and broke your client's jaw." The judge took one last puff, then stabbed out his cigarette. "I'm having you tested."

"For what?"

"Mental illness! I'm sending you to a shrink."

NINE

Last Chance Lassiter

From somewhere in a practice room, a student plucked away on a cello. Or maybe it was just a cat screeching.

I was in the Music Department at the University of Miami. My meeting was with Louis Ciani, a conductor, songwriter, and professor. I'd already given him a cassette of M.C. Silky's *Don't Cry Baby*. Cadillac didn't have a cassette or even an early 45 of *I'm Leaving You, Baby*, so I'd had him play the song into a tape recorder. If Professor Ciani's analysis backed up my client, I'd walk out of here with my expert witness. Unless the scratching cello killed me first.

The professor's office was filled with posters of the New York Philharmonic, the Bolshoi Ballet, and curiously, the Miami Heat. Floor-to-ceiling shelves were packed with books and musical scores. A Sony Walkman sat on his desk. The man himself was in his late fifties with a fine head of white hair tinged nicotine yellow at the temples.

He hovered over a music stand and pointed to a plastic sheet overlay on which he'd written a musical score. "The one on top, that's Silky's *Don't Cry Baby*. The one below is Cadillac's *I'm Leaving You, Baby*, as I've re-created it.

He placed the plastic sheet carefully over the lower score so that certain notes fit identically, one over the other. But to my untrained eye, many other notes did not.

"Silky uses the same musical intervals and rhythmic repetition," Ciani said. "That's the key, and once you combine that with similar lyrics, I can make a good case for plagiarism."

"Great. So you'll testify for me."

"I'll need one of the original 45s to compare to the score."

"Don't have one."

"Surely your client does."

"Cadillac's got nothing from those days. Everything he owned he carried in an Army AWOL bag."

"A collector, then..."

"I've looked online. There are people willing to pay ten grand for an original, but no sellers."

"So where do you go from here?"

"Eddie Burns. Cadillac's old manager is still around. Lives in North Bay Village. He says he's got every master tape from every musician he represented and every song he produced. He's looking for it now."

"When you get it, call me."

Suddenly, the cat-wailing cello down the corridor sounded better to me. "So you'll be our expert?"

"As soon as you pay me a fifteen thousand dollar retainer."

"Ouch. I've got the case on a contingency. No deposit for costs."

"So front the costs. Isn't that what you lawyers do?"

"I'm just out of my own a few days. But you have my word. Win or lose, I'll pay."

Professor Ciani started humming something classical that sounded like Mozart's "Marriage of Figaro." I figured it was his way of thinking out loud.

"You feel strongly about your case, don't you Mr. Lassiter?"

"I feel strongly about my client. Cadillac Johnson is a helluva talented guy who never got a break. I'm his last chance."

"Last Chance Lassiter?"

"For better or worse," I said.

"Can you pay me five now and the ten before trial?"

"I'll find a way. Yeah, I'll do it."

"Then I'm your man."

We shook hands. As I left his office, Professor Ciani was humming again. I couldn't name the song but it sounded joyous, and that was good enough for me.

TEN

The Grilled Cheese Truck

"There are two dozen great restaurants within a few blocks, but you wanted to eat at the grilled cheese truck?" I said.

"You love grilled cheese sandwiches," Kim Coates said.

"Right. I do. But you don't. You like to hit the Biltmore for lunch, when you don't have time to cross the causeway for Joe's."

"I like lunch with you, anywhere."

Okay, so sincerity wasn't one of Kim's strong suits. But after all, she was a lawyer, so her blatant lie was forgivable.

We were standing at the intersection of Brickell Avenue and 10th Street, about a block from Biscayne Bay. A sweet, soft breeze was blowing, but something else was in the wind, and I didn't know what.

"C'mon Kim. What's up?"

"I was a little rough on you the other day."

"Why? Because you broke up with me and called me a loser, and those were the nicest things you said?"

"Oh, Jake." Kim gently touched my cheek, the way you would a baby or lovable puppy. She wore a glen plaid jacket over a black pencil skirt. Professional and sexy at the same time. I wore Miami Dolphins' green polyester shorts and a Marlins' t-shirt. Looking like a beach bum.

"Since you won't answer what we're doing here, let me ask you this, Kim. Are you billing time right now?"

She took a tiny bite of her melted brie on cranberry walnut bread. "Why would you say that?"

"Your firm reps M.C. Silky. You're sitting second chair in a case with me on the other side. You offer to buy me a French onion melt. What do you want?"

"To help you."

I took a healthy bite of the bread, rich with Gruyere and onions. "Okay, help me."

"Silky wants to settle."

My mouth fell open, with a sticky thread of cheese sticking to my lips. "Really? Why?"

"He wants to make a gesture of good will to a legendary musician he admires."

"Let's try it again, this time without the bullshit."

"Krippendorf will fill you in. He'll see us at five."

"Why didn't we go straight there? Why the cheese-covered preview?"

"That was my idea. I don't want you to blow it with Krippendorf. So lose the attitude." She tossed her uneaten sandwich into a garbage can. "And for God's sake, wear a tie."

ELEVEN

Old Meets New

I didn't wear a tie. I wore Miami Dolphins sweat pants and a t-shirt reading: "A Friend Will Help You Move. A Real Friend Will Help You Move a Body." It's one of my favorites.

My client, Cadillac Johnson, wore a tie. A skinny black and gold striped tie made of rayon or acetate, or something that shouted 1959. His shirt was white, his suit black with shiny pants bottoms. His granddaughter Sherrell wore charcoal slacks and a frilly blue silk blouse. She gave me a sharp look when she got off the elevator.

"I don't get your outfit," she said.

"It reinforces Krippendorf's feelings about me."

"And that's good?"

"It also pisses off a woman I used to be involved with."

"And that's good, too?"

"Trust me. It gives me a psychological edge in a room of suits."

I approached the reception desk where Doris Cartwright sat, guarding the door to the interior office.

"Hey Doris," I said. "You miss me?"

"Flag football team does. They've lost every game since you left." She pushed a button on the intercom and informed Krippendorf's assistant that Mr. Lassiter was here with his clients.

A moment later, Cadillac, Sherrell, and I were walking down an interior corridor toward Krippendorf's conference room.

"If they want to settle, that's a good sign, right?" Cadillac asked.

"It means they're afraid of something," I said.

"What?"

"That's what I have to find out before we accept anything."

"Wouldn't it be better to settle and not risk going to court?" Sherrell asked.

"If it's the right amount, yes. But so far, we've gotten no documents, no discovery, no nothing. Not even a notion of how much they'll pay and why. This comes straight out of left field."

We paused in front of the door to the conference room. "I've got arthritis, you know," Cadillac said.

"Yeah?"

"That retirement home down in Kendall. It's got a pool with one of those hot tubs."

"Sounds real nice, Cadillac."

"What Grandad is saying," Sherrell said, "is don't blow this case."

"I get it, Sherrell. I get it."

"They got a Rec Room, too," Cadillac said. "With a little stage up front. The people that run the place said I could put on shows for the folks."

I clasped Cadillac's arm. "Save me a seat in the front row."

We were two steps from the conference room door when I heard the footsteps behind us. Turning, I saw M.C. Silky, wearing a tailored, sleek black sharkskin suit. All his shirts must have been in the laundry, because he wasn't wearing one under his suit coat. Around his neck hung a gold chain big enough to tow an R.V.

Nodding to us and holding up one hand, as if telling us to stop, Silky spoke into a cell phone. This was back in the days of those beige Motorola monstrosities with the rubber aerials. They looked like World War II walkie-talkies and were nearly as heavy.

"John Lee Hooker's tapes?" Silky was saying. "I'll go thirty thousand. What else? The original 'Shake, Rattle and Roll.' Whatever it costs."

He was quiet a moment, listening. "Not Bill Haley! Big Joe Turner."

He clicked off the phone and nodded to Cadillac. "Mr. Johnson, I am privileged to meet you."

The politeness surprised me but didn't seem to move Cadillac.

"How much did you pay for my record?" he demanded.

Silky shrugged. "Wish I could find one. That's a real item. You collect, too?"

"Sure. Social Security."

"Look, man. I really admire you."

"Yeah."

"You guys who crossed over from R and B to rock. You opened all the doors."

"What do you know about it?"

"I know what you think, but I didn't bite your lines."

Cadillac grunted his displeasure.

"I wouldn't copy your stuff 'cause you're better than me."

Silky was trying hard, but Cadillac wouldn't budge.

"Bought me a Tele," Silky said, "but I can't get that twangy sound of yours."

Still the cold shoulder from the old man.

"What'd you play, a Strat?"

"Why?" Cadillac said. "You want to steal my guitar, too?"

Silky laughed and said, "Why don't we all go in? Maybe by the time we're done, we'll all be friends."

Cadillac ignored him and turned to me. "I ain't sitting at the table with this punk ass. Me and Sherrell will be in the lobby. You just do what you think is right."

With that, he turned and Sherrell followed him back down the corridor toward the waiting room.

"Old fool don't know what's good for him," Silky said. "I just hope you do, lawyer man."

TWELVE
See You Bastards in Court

L yle Krippendorf was hunched over his finely polished conference table, scribbling on a legal pad. His prodigious bulk and odd
posture made the pin stripes on his Italian suit as crooked as he was.

"Where's your client?" he said, by way of hello.

"In your waiting room. The air's better there."

Next to the Kripster sat Kim Coates, hands folded in front of
her, hair pulled back into a bun, scowling at me or my outfit, or
both. Next to her, M.C. Silky was just sitting down.

"Here's our starting point," Krippendorf said. "Mr. Silky does
not admit plagiarizing your client's song. In fact, Mr. Silky denies
ever hearing the song until after you filed suit."

"That's hard to believe," I said. "Silky is a collector and very
knowledgeable about R&B and early rock. I can show you a dozen
interviews where he boasts about his knowledge and his collection."

"Does he ever mention your client's song?"

"If he did, we'd already be ringing up the cash register."

"Fine. Prove he heard *I'm Leaving You Baby* or that he read
the score. That's your burden. The song is never played on radio.
The old 45s are nearly impossible to find, and the score was never
published."

"It's still the first quarter of the game, Krip. I've barely begun
discovery."

He smiled like a barracuda. "That's what brings us to this propitious moment. Before each side wastes money on discovery, we're prepared to make a substantial offer to settle your client's claim. Without admitting any infringement, of course. And total confidentiality as to the settlement."

"Just how substantial would that offer be?"

"Seventy-five thousand dollars."

"That's lowball."

"Not where there's no liability."

"A notion I reject. You've got to look at your downside. I have an expert who'll point out all the numerous similarities of the two songs. Then all I have to do is prove Silky had access to *I'm Leaving You, Baby*. Silky's gone platinum. His song – and I say 'his' in the loosest meaning of the word – plays over the opening credits of Tyler Perry's new movie. This case could be worth millions."

Kim Coates looked away, shaking her head. My disappointing her was starting to become a habit.

"Pie in the sky, Lassiter."

"You willing to take that risk?"

"Seventy five thousand is a lot of money to someone in your client's position."

"What position is that? Old? Black? A sucker?"

Kim stirred. "Jake. It's twenty-five thousand in your pocket."

"Really? Call me old fashioned, but I thought lawyers weren't supposed to consider that."

Krippendorf aimed a finger at me. "If I was starting my own shop, I'd take the money and run."

"I'm not you, Krip."

Krippendorf snorted his displeasure.

"I haven't even taken depositions," I said. "Why the rush to settle?"

"Client's idea."

Krippendorf nodded toward Silky, who flashed me his celebrity megawatt smile. "'Cause I respect the old man. Thought I could make his life a little easier is all."

I resisted the urge to get all weak in the knees at the rapper's charitable nature. "Then you wouldn't mind giving a sworn deposition before we accept or reject your offer," I said.

"No way!" Krippendorf thundered, his triple chins quivering. "This is a one-time, pre-discovery offer."

"Then I'll see you bastards in court." My way of combining Sue the Bastards with See You in Court.

Kim spoke up. "Even if you manage to win Jake, which is far-fetched enough, we'd appeal."

"The George Harrison case, where he got sued for 'My Sweet Lord,'" Krippendorf chimed in. "How long did it take?"

"Fifteen years," Kim answered, right on cue. They were tag-teaming me now.

"By then," Krippendorf sniffed, "your client will be worm food."

"You bastard!" I shot back. "That's not what I see when I look at that man sitting in your waiting room in his one good suit."

"Oh, spare us, God, the pious lawyer."

"I see an old man who's depending on me. A man people have screwed over his whole life. And all he wants now is a safe place to live and acknowledgment of the song he wrote, the art he created."

Krippendorf laughed, but it was a dead laugh and his eyes were mirthless. "Is that your idea of lawyering, Lassiter? Breaking out the violins."

"You don't care about justice."

"This is hardball, Lassiter. Care to play?"

"I know your tricks."

"Jake, please stop," Kim pleaded.

I ignored her. "You buy off witnesses, Krippendorf, and you play footsie with judges."

"And you can't cut it, Lassiter. You're an embarrassment."

"You tamper with evidence."

"Better stop right there, fellow."

"You obstruct justice."

"One more word, I'll sue you for slander."

"How about three words? 'You're a pig.'"

"You've got ten seconds to accept the offer or get the hell out."

"I know you, Krip. You never pay a dime, unless you're gonna lose a dollar."

"Five seconds. Four. Three..."

"You know what you can do with your seventy-five thousand?"

"Jake, please," Kim said.

"You horse's ass," Krippendorf added.

"You're your own worst enemy," Kim said, her voice tinged with sadness. "Why can't you bend a little like everybody else?"

"Because I live by no laws but my own," I said, as I stood and headed for the door.

THIRTEEN

A Client's Confidence

In the elevator on the way out of Krippendorf's office building, I told Cadillac and Sherrell that I turned down the seventy-five thousand. Cadillac seemed to suck on his rear teeth while Sherrell started grilling me.

"So we're going to trial?" she asked.

"Damn right. They tried to buy us off."

"I thought that was the idea."

"Actually, they tried to buy me off. Krippendorf thought I'd jump at a quick twenty-five grand. Get my new firm off the ground."

"So Grandad would get an even fifty?"

"Would an apology be coming with that?" Cadillac said.

"Just the opposite. No admission of liability and a confidentiality agreement that would forbid you from even mentioning the case. Silky would own the song like nothing ever happened."

The old man made a rumbling sound in his throat. "That'd be a lie. They'd be paying me to accept that lie."

"Precisely."

Sherrell wouldn't let it go. "If you win in court, Grandad just gets money. There's no apology, right."

"That's right."

"And you could win less than seventy-five thousand."

"Of course."

"Or lose altogether."

"It's possible, but I've got a great expert witness. A professor at U.M. Plus Eddie Burns promises to find the original recording. That's our one-two punch. With them, we'll win a lot more than seventy-five thousand. And when the jury comes back with its number, I want you to watch the look on Silky's face. That'll be all the admission of guilt and all the apology you'll need."

"You're sure about that?" Sherrell asked.

"Yeah, what about it, young man?" Cadillac said. "I'd hate to go through all this and walk away with nothing but a kick in the ass."

I don't like to lie to clients. After all, I warn them about the necessity of telling me the truth. But sometimes clients need bucking up. Their confidence grows shaky. Used to losing, they can't believe they'll finally be the victors.

The ethical rules lawyers are supposed to live by advise us not to guarantee results. There are too many variables to say with certainty how a judge or jury will rule. In addition, the smart guys who write the Bar rules know that a "guarantee" puts the lawyer under pressure to do anything to win, thereby becoming a threat to break other, more substantive rules. But then, as I've said before, I follow my own rules.

"We're gonna win more than seventy-five thousand, Cadillac. I guarantee it."

FOURTEEN
Fight to the Death

I sat on the front porch of Doc Charlie Riggs's sagging house on the edge of the Everglades, taking my old friend's abuse.

"What are you trying to prove, Jake?" Charlie asked. "That you can beat your ex-boss and your ex-girlfriend?"

"That's not it. Krippendorf's hiding something."

"What?"

"No idea."

"Then you should have settled."

"I know the guy, Charlie. He'd never make an offer unless he was afraid of something."

"And you think you can find out."

"That's what I do. It's called lawyering."

Charlie harrumphed and picked up a half-empty bottle of Jack Daniels. He poured a few ounces into a Mason jar and offered me some. I'm a beer guy and shook my head.

"Let's talk about the money," Charlie said. "Let's say for the sake of argument Krippendorf doubled the offer. A hundred fifty thousand. Wouldn't you have to take it?"

"Silky wants a confidentiality agreement and no admission of liability."

"So what?"

"Cadillac would give up all rights to his song. It'd be like *I'm Leaving You, Baby* never existed.

"But he gets the money."

"And loses his legacy. It's not right."

"It's not right to get that old man's hopes up, then lose."

"You want me to compromise, Charlie?"

"Why not?" He took a long pull on his sour mash whiskey. *That's* called lawyering."

"Not my style."

"Sometimes, I think you played football without a helmet, Jake. It's fine to have ideals. Lord knows I've paid a price for sticking to mine. But lawyers live in a gray area, make their living in the shadows."

"This is black and white to me."

"Keep thinking like that, you'll fail. You want to fight to the death, the Krippendorfs of the world will be happy to oblige."

I waited for him to take a long, slow drink, then said, "If you're done criticizing me, I could use some help."

Charlie gave me a crooked smile. "What took you so long to ask?"

FIFTEEN

Shyster vs. Shrink

The psychiatrist's office was in the old DuPont Building in downtown Miami, or as I like to think of it, the City of Lawyers, Pickpockets, Whores, Vultures, and Thieves. The building was the first skyscraper in town, unless you count the courthouse, which in my line of work, you ought to count.

The seventeen-story DuPont dates from the late 1930s, its architecture called "Depression Moderne." It's a limestone edifice with bas relief elevator doors, brass gates, Cypress ceilings and marble floors and balustrades. But those are the public areas. The office of psychiatrist Dr. Moira Golden was jammed against the elevator shaft on the 12th floor and occupied a cramped, dimly lit space of musty carpets and mismatched African art. It was enough to make a guy depressed.

Judge Buckstrom had ordered me to be evaluated by Dr. Golden. I briefly wondered whether a finding of insanity would help my defense. Probably not. The boys in Tallahassee don't need any psychopaths on the team roster. I decided to play it right down the middle and be myself, which is to say, a calm man of pleasant disposition, who cannot be ruffled or flustered by insult or injury.

"You don't want to be here, do you, Mr. Lassiter?" Dr. Golden asked.

"Hell, no. Who would?"

I made a mental note to lower my voice.

Moira Golden was in her early forties, an attractive brunette a bit broad in the beam, perhaps from sitting all day long. She had expensively manicured nails of a turquoise color, which I found distracting. She took notes on a legal pad, which made me feel right at home.

"I want you to watch something and get your reaction," Dr. Golden said.

"Whatever you say, Doc."

She punched a button on a remote and fired up a VCR. In a couple of seconds, the television came to life with a video clip of an old football game. I didn't have to be told it was the Dolphins versus the Jets at the old Shea Stadium in New York. A cold, foggy, snowy day. Misery was in the air on that Sunday afternoon about a million years ago.

The Dolphins had just scored and were kicking off, which meant that if you looked very closely, you could see number 58 on the suicide squad, hopping up and down, trying to stay warm and stir up the blood for a vicious hit. Number 58, you see, was me.

The kickoff was short, reaching the twenty or so, and the Jets' return man caught it in full stride. I was moving fast, too, and the blocker assigned to put me on his ass slipped on the icy field, and I shot past him.

The collision occurred near the Jets' thirty-five yard line. My form was perfect. Head-up, legs churning, shoulders aimed at the returner's sternum. We crashed into each other, an explosion I felt from my teeth to my tailbone. At first I wasn't even aware that the ball had squirted loose, sailing over my head and skittering across the icy field.

"Ball! Ball! Ball!"

It was one of my teammates, telling the troops that a fumble was there for the taking. One of the Jets' blockers had a clean shot but couldn't control the slippery spheroid. Two of my fellow Dolphins knocked each other off the ball. The kicker had a shot, but he wasn't about to get pounced on by a ton of beef, so he sashayed toward the sideline.

Somehow – I don't know how – I had gotten up and galloped toward the action. And there it was, the ball, spinning across the ground at my feet. Did I mention I suffered a concussion making the tackle? No matter. In those days, fretting over head injuries was for sissies.

I scooped the ball up and was immediately hit by one of the Jets' reserve running backs, who doubled as a blocker on the kick-return team. He couldn't tackle for shit, and I swatted him off me. Another hit and I was knocked sideways, bracing a hand against the ground. Then, suddenly, I was running and on the video, the announcer was screaming.

"Lassiter has the ball and he's taking off! The wrong way! The wrong way! He's headed for the Dolphins' end zone."

My teammates were chasing me and yelling what I thought was encouragement. I reached the end zone and tossed the ball into the lower deck. A safety. Two points for the Jets, and we lost the game by one. The headline the next day read: "Wrong-Way Lassiter Dooms Fins."

Dr. Golden fast-forwarded through a commercial until she got to the instant replay. "Look at that!" the play-by-play announcer shouted. "Lassiter's knee was clearly down after he recovered the fumble. It should have been the Dolphins' ball at that spot on the field."

These were the days before coaches could challenge officials' calls, so all the replays in the world couldn't change the outcome.

"Watching that now, Mr. Lassiter, what do you think?"

"I run like a drunk stomping grapes."

"What I mean is, how do you feel about such a public humiliation?"

"I was robbed. You saw the replay. I recovered the fumble and should have been ruled down by contact."

"So the system didn't treat you fairly?"

"That's one way to put it."

"Your team lost and you were held up to scorn and ridicule. How do you feel about that?"

"What do you want me to say? Angry? Violent? Insane?"

"If that's how you feel."

"I was pissed. I still am. I walk into a bar, and some fat turd calls me 'Wrong-Way Lassiter.' But I don't punch the guy out."

"Are you saying you'd like to?"

"No. Jeez, don't put words in my mouth."

Dr. Golden scribbled a note on her pad.

"What are you writing?"

"Not your concern, Wrong-Way. Do you get 'pissed' when I call you that?"

"Aw, this is bullshit." I stirred in my chair as if to get up.

"If you leave, I'll have to tell Judge Buckstrom that you're uncooperative and having difficulty controlling your anger."

"I'm not angry, goddamit!"

"Be honest, Wrong-Way? When I call you that, you want to hit me, don't you?"

"My Granny taught me that only low-life scumbags ever hit a woman."

"How do you think failing so spectacularly on national television affected you?"

"You're the shrink. You tell me."

"I think it fits a pattern. You feel the system failed you, just as it did your friend, the former medical examiner."

"What do you know about that?"

"Enough to know you were on the wrong side."

"Charlie Riggs got hosed because the boys downtown thought he should roll over for the state and not be impartial."

Dr. Golden took some more notes. That probably shouldn't have irritated me, but it did. I felt that, no matter what she was writing down, it would be damaging. Why did the judge pick this monster to examine me? Was there a conspiracy to bring me down? Or was I being paranoid? Maybe I should ask the shrink.

"So you rebel against the system, Wrong Way," she said. "You purposely flout the rules."

"Basically, I just live by my own." Forcing myself to remain calm.

That prompted yet more note taking.

"What is it you want for yourself, Wrong Way?"

The question stopped me. It's not something I think much about. But the answer was there, honest and true. I wanted the same thing for myself I did for Doc Charlie Riggs and Cadillac Johnson, and everyone else who's been fucked over.

"I just want a second chance," I said.

SIXTEEN

Wrong-Way Lassiter

The iron gate outside Eddie Burns' bayside home was emblazoned with a treble clef. The place was on Treasure Drive just off the 79th Street Causeway, a North Bay Village mini-manse with floor-to-ceiling glass overlooking Biscayne Bay. Eddie Burns wore a blue blazer with gold buttons, a paisley ascot, white linen pants, and white patent leather loafers with no socks. His ankles were lined with purple veins. He looked to be somewhere between 80 and purgatory.

At the moment, he was shaking some bitters into a cocktail glass. He'd already poured bourbon over ice, added a hint of water and sugar, and then plopped a maraschino cherry on top.

It had been a while since I'd had a maraschino cherry in a drink. But then, I don't usually sit around at 11 a.m. drinking Old-Fashioneds with Eddie Burns.

Twenty-four hours ago, I'd spoken to Eddie on the phone. He'd found the master tape of *I'm Leaving You, Baby*, as recorded by Cadillac Johnson in 1959. It was a crucial piece of evidence.

"So kid, you know how Cadillac got his name?" Eddie asked.

I shrugged in the direction of Frank Sinatra, or rather his autographed photo on the wall. "Ring a Ding Ding, Eddie," it said.

"I owned this red Eldo ragtop," Eddie continued. "Cadillac would run his hand over the upholstery like he was stroking a broad's ass."

A broad, I thought. I half expected Sinatra to be singing *The Lady is a Tramp* in the background.

"Cadillac liked the Eldo so much, I bought him one just like mine. That's the kind a guy I am, Lassiter."

Burns pulled a Torpedo, the huge Cuban cigar, from his blazer pocket, and lit up. He seemed damned satisfied with himself.

"The way I heard it, Mr. Burns, you bought the Caddy wholesale and deducted the retail price from Cadillac's royalties."

Burns waved his giant cigar as if the smoke could obscure all notions of his sleaziness. "Musicians been complaining about their managers since Dick Clark was in diapers. I never took the copyrights like Irv Mills did with Duke Ellington or Phil Spector with the Ronettes."

"You sound regretful about that."

"Hell, no, I love Cadillac too much for that." He blew some cigar smoke my way. "But had I taken the copyrights, you'd be representing me against M.C. Silky. Wouldn't that be something?"

Burns moved to a piano, sat down, played the first few bars of *I'm Leaving You, Baby*, and warbled the lyrics in a scratchy voice.

"I'm leaving you baby...
Don't ask why.
I'm leaving you baby...
Baby, baby, baby don't cry."

"So could I get the master tape from you?" I asked, when he had finished.

"Wish I could."

"What's that mean?"

"You're a day late. And *mucho dinero* short. I sold it yesterday."

"Sold it! What bullshit is that?"

"It's the *emmis*. Young guy in a dark suit. Said he was a collector. Paid fifty thousand cash."

"That's no collector! He's gotta be one of Krippendorf's dwarves."

"Who?"

"Some kid lawyer who's working for Silky's firm. Stealing the evidence so they can deep six it."

"He didn't steal anything. He bought it."

"From you, Eddie! You just helped the enemy!"

"That's life, kid."

"What about, 'I love Cadillac?' You son-of-a-bitch!"

"You're kind of new at this, aren't you, Lassiter? The guy with the cash always wins."

"Bullshit."

"The strong, the fast, the rich. They're the winners. Guys like Cadillac Johnson, losers all the way."

"You're a heartless bastard."

"Cadillac thought his talent was enough. That he'd keep on writing and singing and recording. That he didn't have to take crap from shit-bird promoters. The man never learned how to kiss ass."

"Funny, me neither."

"So look at him now. What's he got? *Bupkes*! Nothing is what he's got."

"Ever stop to think you might bear some responsibility for that?"

"Anyone ever call you naive?"

"That and a lot worse."

Burns tapped ashes from his phallic cigar and said, "I was there that day."

"What day?"

He tapped out a tune on the piano and started singing:

"Buy me some peanuts and cracker jacks,

I don't care if we never get back."

"I don't know what you're talking about," I said.

"'Wrong Way Lassiter. The day you scored for the other team."

"That's a football story, and you're singing a baseball song."

"Poetic license, Lassiter. Besides, ain't no good football songs."

I didn't know what point he was making, other than trying to embarrass me.

"I was living in New York then," he said. "Had Jets' season tickets."

"Congratulations. I hope you got frostbite."

"I watched the whole play through binoculars."

"So?"

"When you recovered the fumble, your knee was down by contact. The play was dead right there, or should have been."

"I know. So what?"

"Bad call cost the Dolphins the game and made you look like a fool."

"Okay. What's your point?"

"What I'm saying goes for you and Cadillac and the whole damn world. Life ain't fair, kid. Life ain't fucking fair."

■ ■ ■

To the west, over the Everglades, a thunderstorm was brewing. I was in my ancient Olds 442 convertible, chugging down I-95, when my cell phone rang. I owned a Motorola 8000X, an analog phone, just like Michael Douglas in the original "Wall Street." Coverage was so sketchy, I was as likely to pick up Launch Control at Cape Canaveral as my secretary in Miami Beach. I muscled the phone – heavy as a small bar bell – to my ear.

"How'd it go with Eddie Burns?" Cece asked.

"You first. What's up?"

"Bad news, *jefe*."

"Now what?"

"Professor Ciani flipped. He's on their witness list. Gonna testify for Silky."

"That son-of-a-bitch! Eddie Burns sold us out, too."

They say bad news comes in threes, I thought. What would come next? In the distance, lightning flashed, and the phone line crackled. "Anything else, Cece?"

I heard papers rustling over the phone, or maybe that was just static on the line.

"A messenger just delivered a motion for summary judgment from Krippendorf's office. Affidavits, exhibits, a demand the case be dismissed. Hearing's next week."

"Great. Just great."

"We gotta come forward with evidence or it's over."

"Thanks, Cece, but I know what a summary judgment motion is."

"Then you've got evidence, right Jake?"

"Sure I do, Cece."

I hung up, thinking I had the same thing as Cadillac.

Bupkes!

SEVENTEEN

Hitting the Chords

I was flipping burgers on the backyard grill while a worried Warren Zevon was singing. Seems he was gambling in Havana and lost big-time.

"Send lawyers, guns and money...
The shit has hit the fan."

Yeah, I can relate.

Some lawyers meet their clients in the Bankers Club in a downtown high-rise with views extending as far as Bimini. Stone crabs and sliced tenderloin, gin and tonics, or just passion-fruit iced tea if important business is to be discussed.

Me? If like the clients, I invite them over to the house for beer and burgers. I live in a little coral rock house between Poinciana and Kumquat in Coconut Grove. It has stood up to numerous hurricanes and more than a few raucous parties during my playing days and a fewer number during my lawyering days.

Tonight, with burgers grilling and Grolsch flowing, Cadillac and Sherrell were my guests, and while they enjoyed my hospitality, they weren't especially thrilled with my professional services.

"Grandad, we got a big hero for a lawyer." The sarcasm in Sherrell's voice was as tangy as the soy-pineapple marinade I use on the burgers. "He turns down the money because he's got this great case. But then, he loses his witnesses!"

"Sherrell, mind your manners," Cadillac instructed.

She lowered her voice into some approximation of my own: "'We're gonna win more than seventy-five thousand, Cadillac. I guarantee it.' Bullshit!"

"It's not over," I reminded her.

"I should report you to the Bar."

"You'll have to take a number."

"Great to learn that now. Why didn't you tell us what a fuck-up you were when I first came in?"

"Listen, Sherrell, once I find what Silky is hiding—"

"How? You can't even keep your own witnesses honest!"

"By playing by Krippendorf's rules, which is to say, no rules at all."

"Really? He's better at it than you, which is probably why he recommended you in the first place." She wheeled away from the grill where I was intent on keeping our burgers bloody. Cadillac sat at an old redwood picnic table, holding his acoustic guitar. He'd been strumming and humming earlier, but Sherrell's outburst had dampened the mood.

"I don't blame you, Jake," Cadillac said, gently. "I don't blame Eddie Burns or even that shyster Krippendorf. I should have paid better attention to my business affairs and my personal affairs. When I slid downhill, there wasn't nobody pushing me from behind."

"But my job is to catch you," I told him. "I made promises to you, and I intend to keep them."

Cadillac picked up his guitar and seemed to contemplate just what notes to play. "There's a moment in time when you stand at a crossroads. A man can go either way." He strummed a major chord.

"Top of the highest mountain."

Then hit a minor chord.

"Or bottom of the deepest pit."

"It's my job to make sure you get back what you lost," I said.

"Get me my due."

"That's right."

"Before I turn to dust, young man, I'd like credit for what I've done."

This time, he hit a bluesy chord and said, "What's a man got, anyway, but his name?"

EIGHTEEN

Games Lawyers Play

In depositions, as in football, you crave home field advantage.

If I'm taking a witness's sworn pre-trial statement, I want to do it in my office. Or at least, I did, before I moved my meager belongings to the parking garage in the alley. So when Lyle Krippendorf suggested that we use his quarters for Professor Ciani's deposition, I agreed.

"I think you'll agree, Jake, that we'll all be more comfortable in my conference room. We can stretch out, bring lunch in, and you can take all day if you want."

Translation: I know you're embarrassed by that hellhole you're renting, and I don't want to inhale exhaust fumes all afternoon, so I'll spring for some deli and you can spread your files on my mahogany table and see what you're missing.

I knew it wouldn't take all afternoon. Professor Ciani betrayed me for a payday, and there was no way to turn that around. But I could chisel away at his testimony and pin him to a position I could then attack at trial.

Once pleasantries had been exchanged and coffee poured, the court reporter administered the oath, and I let Ciani blather on a bit about his degrees and his work as a composer. Yes, he'd testified in other cases. No, he was not a friend of either M.C. Silky or anyone in the Krippendorf firm. No, in his expert opinion, Silky did not plagiarize Cadillac's work.

I placed the plastic overlay of Silky's score over Cadillac's older song. Then throwing Ciani's own words from our first meeting back at him, I asked, "Isn't it true Silky's *Don't Cry, Baby* uses the same musical intervals and rhythmic repetition as Cadillac's *I'm Leaving You, Baby?*"

"Partially true," which I figured was an apt description of much of Ciani's testimony.

"What part is true and what part is not?" I was trying not to sound pissed.

"In a nutshell, the differences are greater than the similarities."

"But you would concede there are similarities both in the music and the lyrics?"

"Not sufficient to indicate plagiarism because of the combination of different musical elements."

"Such as?"

"Silky's staccato phrasing is different than your client's soul inflection. Silky's rap beat is different than your client's beat. I could go on."

"Please do."

"Why don't I just sum it up? The songs are clearly different."

"Despite similar notes?"

"Yes."

"And similar rhythmic repetitions?"

"Yes."

"And musical intervals."

"Objection, repetitious," Krippendorf said.

"You may answer, Professor Ciani," I said. "Mr. Krippendorf is just letting me know he's still awake."

"Let me put it this way. Unlike words, there are fewer combinations of notes. Sooner or later, practically every motif will be repeated, without any copying or plagiarism."

That one stung. But the answer served a purpose. It laid out the defense. Cadillac's song lacked uniqueness. Therefore, someone repeating its patterns and notes decades later might not necessarily be guilty of plagiarism.

"Isn't it true you expressed a different opinion when you met with me?" I asked.

"As I recall, I expressed certain preliminary thoughts but had not yet studied the matter in depth."

"So your opinion then about the songs' similarities was only preliminary?"

"So preliminary as to not even be an opinion. More of a notion."

I suppressed the urge to strangle the professor and simply asked, "Are you being paid for your testimony today?"

"I'm being paid to render an impartial expert opinion."

Crafty, I'll give him that.

"And how much does it cost to extract that impartial opinion from you?"

"A retainer of twenty thousand dollars to be earned at the rate of four hundred dollars per hour."

Pretty good money for those days. No wonder he switched sides before I could officially retain him.

"Any more questions, Jake?" Krippendorf asked.

"Many. Why do you ask?"

"Because you stopped and you look perturbed."

"I don't get perturbed, Krip. Sometimes, I get pissed. I might even get mad as hell. But I don't get perturbed."

"There's no need to use that threatening tone of voice."

The son-of-a-bitch was baiting me. "My voice is the same tone it is when ordering a Grolsch at the Barristers' Saloon. You got a problem with that, Krip?"

"Let the record reflect that Mr. Lassiter has raised his voice in an attempt to intimidate the witness."

I felt like picking up one of the corned beef sandwiches on the deli platter and squashing it in Krippendorf's face, but I knew that's the kind of stunt he hoped I'd pull.

"The only thing that intimidates your witness is the prospect of working for less than four hundred bucks an hour."

"I resent that insinuation," Professor Ciani said.

"Tough shit," I said.

"Let the record reflect that Mr. Lassiter is now using scatological terms in an affront to the dignity of the court," Krippendorf said.

"The record speaks – and smells – for itself," I said.

"That's it!" Krippendorf slammed his legal pad onto his fine mahogany table. "This deposition is terminated."

NINETEEN

Singing for Judge and Jury

I lay in the hammock in the backyard, rocking to and fro, occasionally sipping at a 16-ounce Grolsch, the green bottle with the porcelain stopper.

Lawyer at Work.

Really.

Doc Charlie Riggs was there, drinking Jack Daniels from a tumbler, seeing how I had no Mason jars in the house. A coroner by training, he'd spent more time in courtrooms than most trial lawyers, so I valued his instincts and his expertise. Charlie loved reading appellate court opinions, sometimes mocking the logic, but always lending insight to my trial preparation. At the moment, he was reading *Arnstein versus Porter*, an opinion of the Second Circuit Court of Appeals.

"Cole Porter got sued for plagiarism," Charlie mused. "Now there's an oldie."

"But a goodie. Stands for the proposition a plaintiff doesn't need an expert witness to prove plagiarism. And guess what? I don't have one."

"What else don't you have?"

"The original score and recording by Cadillac. In fact, I don't have any recording. *I'm Leaving You, Baby* is a collectors' items so rare I can't lay my hands on a record."

"How is that possible?"

"Cece located five old 45s, pretty much spread across the country. Three were owned by dealers. By the time we called, they'd each just sold them to the same guy, with delivery to a P.O. Box in Jacksonville."

"Jacksonville?"

"Krippendorf has a satellite office there. So I figure..."

"He has a beard collecting and deep-sixing every 45 he can find."

I nodded and so did my Grolsch bottle. "The buyer's name – Avery Goodblatt – doesn't match anyone in the firm. It could be his boat captain or personal trainer, but most likely it's just a P.I. using phony I.D. We can't locate the guy anywhere."

"What about the other two 45s?"

"Owned by personal collectors. One wouldn't talk to us. The other had just sold his copy to Mr. Avery Goodblatt."

"Shipped to a post office box in Jacksonville?"

"Yep."

Charlie sipped at his Jack Daniels, savored the taste, then said, "Cadillac still own a guitar?"

"Sure."

"Can he still sing?"

"Like an angel with the blues."

"Isn't that your answer then? You put Cadillac under oath. He swears he wrote and recorded *I'm Leaving You, Baby*, in 1959 or whenever. Then he plays and sings the song for judge and jury."

"After the applause dies down, then what?"

"What do you think?"

That was just like Doc Riggs. Always making me think for myself. "I don't know. That's why I'm asking."

"What is it you lack?"

"An expert witness. Oh! There it is. While Cadillac is on the stand, I play Silky's *Don't Cry, Baby*. I'll have him dissect both songs."

"Exactly. Who's a better expert witness than the man who wrote the first song?"

"Of course, they'll impeach Cadillac as having an interest in the case. But we impeach experts all the time for being paid whores for one side or the other." I drained the beer, thought everything over, and said, "Not bad, Charlie, and in reality, I have no other choices."

I swung out of the hammock to pull a fresh Grolsch from a picnic cooler. Charlie smacked his lips with satisfaction, or maybe that's how he always sounded after a swig of sour mash whiskey.

"What about proving access to Cadillac's song?" Charlie asked. "Will Silky admit having heard it?"

"He professes to love Cadillac's work but swears under oath he never heard *I'm Leaving You, Baby.*"

"Can you prove he's lying?"

"Nope. Which means, without access, I have a higher burden of proof. I have to show the songs are not just similar but, what the hell's the legal term, really similar?"

"That's not a legal term," Charlie said.

"I know. I just can't remember the magic language in the appellate cases."

"A plaintiff need not prove access where the songs are so similar 'as to preclude independent creation.'"

"That's it, Charlie."

"Or so said the judges in *Heim versus United Music.*"

"Now you're showing off. But you're right. That's the burden of proof when a plaintiff can't prove the defendant heard the copyrighted song."

"What about Professor Ciani?"

"He'll say the songs aren't that similar. That it's just a motif being repeated at random."

"Not good."

"Ciani's the ball game. If I can't discredit him, I lose."

Charlie thought that over a moment, his thinking process lubricated by the last of the Jack Daniels. "If only you could prove Silky had the old record..."

"Yeah?"

"You'd lower your burden of proof on plagiarism, but just as important, you'd show Silky lied under oath."

"And if he lied about one thing..."

"Exactly. It's a virtual guarantee the jury would find he's also lying about not copying the song. Slam-dunk automatic win for the good guys."

"Right on all counts, Charlie. But how do I prove he had the record or at least heard it?"

"How the hell should I know? You're the lawyer."

TWENTY

The Summons

I was jogging down the bike path along Old Cutler Road a few blocks south of the Gables Waterway, when the midnight black BMW convertible cut me off. Behind the wheel was Kim Coates. We hadn't spoken since the aborted settlement conference. My instincts told me that she'd seen me jogging and just pulled over to say hello, maybe throw her arms around me, tell me how much she missed me and what a fool she'd been.

My instincts were wrong.

The car was idling in the shade of a banyan tree when I approached the driver's door and gave her a sweaty smile. "Kim, what's up?"

She slid the window down but made no move to get out. Instead, she handed me a legal-size envelope. "You're going to want to read this," she said.

"If it's another settlement proposal, you could have just picked up the phone."

Once again, my instincts were wrong.

"You've been served," she said in a voice devoid of emotion.

"What?"

"James Farrell versus Jacob Lassiter. Assault and battery and intentional infliction of emotional distress."

"Emotional distress, my ass!"

"Calm down, Jake."

74

I leaned into the open window, and she recoiled. Either she thought I was going to bite her nose off or I smelled bad. Or both. A young couple on a two-person bike pedaled by. "You're representing that slime against me?"

"He hired the firm. Krippendorf assigned me the case."

"He's a sadist. Don't you get that?"

"I had no choice, Jake."

"You always have a choice!"

I tore open the envelope and thumbed through the summons and complaint, stopping at the *ad damnum* clause. "Five hundred thousand dollars? I'll let him punch me for a half a million bucks!"

"What if I could make it go away?"

"How?"

Instead of answering, she just looked at me. The look a teacher gives to a particularly slow student.

"Oh shit, Kim. If I tank Cadillac's case, you'll get me off the hook with Farrell. Is that the deal?"

"You're not giving up anything. You're going to lose Cadillac's case anyway."

"So why'd you offer to settle? Why the seventy-five grand?"

"Strictly the client's idea."

"So why not just sue me for the half million I don't have?"

She reached out through the window and stroked my cheek. "Because I care about you."

"Uh-huh."

"And I don't want to see you get hurt."

"Right."

Her fingers crept around the back of my neck and played at the hairline. That kiss I'd predicted seemed to be in the offing. "And I miss you."

I pulled away. "You'll get over it."

I started running south, toward Matheson Hammock, sneakers pounding the pavement, but not loud enough to drown out her voice. "You're a sorry-ass loser, Jake! That's why I dumped you."

TWENTY-ONE

Welcome, Truth Seekers

I did not have time to worry about Farrell's lawsuit against me.

Or the disbarment proceeding.

Or whether my bougainvilleas were getting enough water.

I was in trial in the county courthouse downtown. Or rather in a hearing before Judge Willard Colton on Krippendorf's motion for summary judgment. If I lost, there would be no trial, and a jury would never hear the case.

A black vulture was perched on the limestone ledge outside the courthouse window. Two more soared in the updrafts. Maybe they were the same ones that parasailed outside Krippendorf's high-rise offices, or they could just be cousins.

The computer printout at the door to the courtroom read: "William Johnson, a/k/a Cadillac Johnson vs. Percival Morton a/k/a M.C. Silky."

Percival?

Then there was this sign above the judge's bench: "We Who Labor Here Seek Only the Truth."

What a crock!

It's part of our cultural heritage. We believe we have the best legal system in the gosh-darned world. To which I reply, What about trial by battle?

We believe that justice will prevail, and I say, Only if it has more money.

We believe that judges protect the weak from the strong. But I say listen to the down-and-out lawyer played by Paul Newman in "The Verdict" when he angrily tells the judge: "I know about you. You couldn't hack it as a lawyer. You were a bag man for the boys downtown, and you still are."

Now back to that sign. "We Who Labor Here Seek Only the Truth."

I've said it before and I'll say it again. There ought to be a footnote. Subject to the truth being concealed by lying witnesses, distorted by sleazy lawyers, and excluded by inept judges."

With that thought echoing in my brain, I went to court.

■ ■ ■

Cadillac Johnson sat on the witness stand, strumming his guitar and singing.

"I'm leaving you, baby.
Got to say goodbye.
I'm leaving you, baby.
Don't ask why."

Judge Colton had cut me one small break. Ordinarily, motions for summary judgment are decided on the paperwork. No witnesses testify, except by affidavit. If the evidence and facts overwhelmingly favor the moving party – in this case Silky – so that a jury could not legally find for the other party, the motion is granted. The judge was going to listen to both songs. Krippendorf had submitted a tape of *Don't Cry, Baby.* I had no tape, score, or vinyl, so the judge allowed Cadillac to perform live.

In one respect, it was a victory for the good guys. On the other hand, the judge was just covering his ass. If he ruled against us, the appellate court couldn't overturn on the basis he didn't give us a fair hearing.

The judge thumbed through Professor Ciani's musical score overlays – and his affidavit asserting no plagiarism – while Silky's tape played.

"Don't cry, baby.

You my sexy lady.

Don't cry, baby.

Baby, baby, baby."

The judge called for a fifteen minute recess so he could consider the issues alone in chambers. I figured he either needed to call his bookie or take a dump. Either way, he returned to the bench, as promised, and spent roughly ninety seconds in silence, trying to appear judicial but succeeding only in driving up my blood pressure.

Colton was a heavyset man in his fifties with flowing silvery hair. He'd been a prosecutor in the State Attorney's office for twenty-five years. A lifer. After serving on several Florida Bar committees that re-write the Rules of Criminal Procedure – a task no sane man would undertake – and contributing some dough to the state Republican Party, Colton was appointed by the Governor to fill the unexpired term of a judge who landed in prison for offering to sell the names of confidential informants to various hit men. Miami Justice, I like to call it.

Judge Colton cleared his throat with a judicial *har-rumph*, nodded to the court stenographer, and began in stentorian tones: "The Court finds that the plaintiff has proved the two songs are similar and rejects the defense argument that, as a matter of probabilities, nearly every musical phrase will be repeated without plagiarism."

So far, so good. Next to me at the defense table, Sherrell Johnson was latched onto my forearm in a death grip. Cadillac seemed relaxed. I figured the old guy had been in tougher spots.

"However..." the judge continued.

I hate the word *however*.

"The plaintiff has failed to prove – or to create a triable issue – that the defendant had access to the first song."

"Your Honor," I said, getting to my feet. "Under *Heim versus United Music–*"

"Let me finish, Mr. Lassiter. The songs are not so strikingly similar as to allow the Court to infer access under the Heim case."

Now, Cadillac stirred in his seat. "You saying that punk didn't steal my music, judge?"

"I'm saying your lawyer hasn't proved Mr. Silky even heard your music."

"Hasn't proved it yet, Your Honor," I said. "If you let this case go to trial, we'll have sufficient time to prove it up. Mr. Krippendorf set this motion on short notice, and we haven't had the opportunity to fully develop the evidence."

"Then let me help you out," the judge said. "Mr. Silky, have you ever owned a recording of the plaintiff's song?"

"No, sir," Silky said, from the defense table.

"Ever hear his song before you wrote your own?"

"Objection to the phrase 'your own,'" I said.

"Overruled. Mr. Silky?"

"I don't believe so, Judge. At least, I can't remember ever hearing it."

The judge turned back to me with a self-satisfied look. "As I said, Mr. Lassiter, there's no proof of access."

I slid out from behind the plaintiff's table, took three steps and planted myself like an oak in front of the bench. "Your Honor, if you don't mind my saying so, you take a lousy deposition."

"Sit down, Mr. Lassiter."

"You couldn't bust a Girl Scout for possession of cookies."

"I'm warning you..."

I didn't sit down. Didn't move a millimeter. "Now, maybe I don't play golf with you, or contribute to your campaigns...."

"Careful, Mr. Lassiter."

I heard a Krippendorfian chuckle coming from the defense table,

"But I know my rights," I continued.

"Got your toothbrush in that briefcase? Because you're this close to being held in contempt." The judge held his thumb and forefinger an inch apart.

"Is that the size of your brain or your penis?" I fired back.

The judge's neck turned red. "You apologize this instant!"

It was the first time anyone demanded an apology from me since I punched out James Farrell and Krippendorf was all over my ass. Which, come to think of it, wasn't that long ago.

I stayed silent.

"Mr. Lassiter! Are you going to apologize?"

"No way."

"No way? Wrong Way! No wonder they call you that. You are hereby—"

"I move to recuse on the ground of bias."

"Denied!"

"Move for a hearing on bias."

"Denied!"

"Move for an adjournment."

"Denied!"

"Fine. Do what you want. I'll appeal your ass all the way to—"

The judge banged his gavel, the echo ricocheting like a rifle shot through the courtroom. "You are hereby held in direct contempt of court. Bailiff, escort Mr. Lassiter to the lock-up."

The bailiff was the uncle of the Chief Deputy Clerk. He was a jangly-jointed man in a baggy uniform who looked fearful as he approached me. As if I might give him a forearm shiver. But I fell in step with him, turning only to Cadillac and Sherrell and saying, "It ain't over. Not by a long shot."

TWENTY-TWO
Set the Shyster Free

I t was just after sundown when three burly corrections officers began the dangerous task of transporting me from the courthouse lock-up to the county jail. I guess they thought two weren't enough.

My hands were cuffed behind my back, but I was spared the indignity of leg irons, a blindfold, and a gag. We had just exited the courthouse onto Flagler Street where a sheriff's van was parked. Which is when my hero arrived.

Doc Charlie Riggs wasn't riding a white horse. He squealed to the curb in a muddy Dodge pick-up and hopped out, waving a piece of paper.

"Unhand that man!" he demanded, somewhat archaically.

They did no such thing. One of the officers examined the paper. It wasn't a court order, but rather a handwritten note on Judge Colton's personal stationery. The puzzled lawman read aloud: "The contempt citation against Attorney Jacob Lassiter is hereby rescinded and he may go forth henceforth as a free man."

"What the fuck?" the officer said.

"Henceforth," I said, cheerfully.

"That ain't official," the other officer said.

"I just came from Judge Colton's house," Doc Riggs said. "He asked to be called to confirm the authenticity of his order."

Doc Riggs offered the first officer his cell phone. His face registering skepticism, the officer dialed the number emblazoned in fancy script on the judge's stationery, then walked off a few paces and had a conversation out of earshot. When he returned, he said to one of his cohorts: "Set the shyster free."

■■■

"You want to tell me how you did this?" I asked.

Doc Riggs sipped at his Jack Daniels. "Nope."

We were sitting on adjacent bar stools at a downtown watering hole, just minutes after my release. "You went to the judge's house?" I asked.

"Lovely Mediterranean architecture. Near the Biltmore just off Anastasia."

"I'm assuming you weren't carrying a bag full of cash."

"Didn't need to. I just called in an old debt."

I took a pull on my beer and spent a moment trying to figure what the judge could owe the former Medical Examiner and came up blank.

"As long as we're playing Twenty Questions, let me ask how old that old debt is?"

"Back before Colton was a judge."

"Okay. He was in the state attorney's office. Deputy Chief of Homicide. You were M.E. What could he owe you?"

"None of your business."

"You didn't lie for him on the stand, did you?"

"Screw you, Jake! You know me better than that."

"What then? He's a necrophiliac and you provided him bodies."

Doc Riggs took a long drink of his sour mash whiskey. "Close, but no cigar."

"What? Now you gotta tell me."

Doc Riggs sighed and said, "Long time ago, Colton was seeing a young C.S.I. on the side, and I covered for him. Hell, I gave him the spare office in the morgue where I kept a cot and a liquor cabinet. Colton would tell his wife he had to watch an autopsy or meet with one of the deputy examiners, and if she drove by the morgue, sure enough, his car would be there. He always told me if I needed anything, not to hesitate to ask."

"And tonight you asked."

Doc Riggs drained the rest of his drink and motioned the bartender for another. "I told him you weren't quite the horse's ass you often appear to be, and you really believe in your client's case."

"Yeah?"

"Colton won't enter an order dismissing Cadillac's suit for 72 hours, and he's ordering Silky to give you a full deposition. If you come up with any evidence he had access to Cadillac's song, he'll deny the summary judgment and let the case go to trial."

"Holy shit."

"I assume that's your way of saying 'thank you.'"

"Thank you, Charlie."

"You're welcome."

"Why didn't you reach into your bag of tricks before I got thrown in the can?"

"I was hoping you wouldn't need extra-curricular help."

"I *always* need help. But now, we're gonna win this thing."

"Don't start celebrating yet. How do you know Silky's lying when he says he never heard the song?"

"I know it in my bones. We've been over this. Silky's a major collector of early rock and roll. He's got 45s of all of Cadillac's contemporaries. Why doesn't he have any of Cadillac's songs? Especially his most famous? It doesn't compute."

"Okay. Say you're right. How do you crack him?"

I took a handful of peanuts and tossed them in my mouth. As I chewed, I said, "I've spent the last several hours in a jail cell thinking about that."

"And...?"

"I'm sure Silky is hiding the record. All I have to do is find it."

"And how do you propose to do that?"

"Simple, Charlie. I have to make him move it, and be there when he does."

TWENTY-THREE
Rage Control

"**M**r. Lassiter is an agnostic lawyer," Dr. Moira Golden said.

"Meaning what?" Judge Willard Buckstrom asked.

"He doesn't believe the concept of justice exists. Or at the very least, he strongly doubts it."

I fidgeted in my chair. I should be taking M.C. Silky's deposition, but instead, I was trapped in Judge Buckstrom's chambers where Dr. Golden was delivering her report on my mental status. Seated around the long conference table were my antagonists. James Farrell, his jaw no longer wired shut, glared at me. Kim Coates made eye contact with a look that could only be called rehearsed concern. Florida Bar investigator George Grumley scribbled notes furiously, hoping to hear something that would justify pulling my ticket to practice law.

"Mr. Lassiter believes passionately in his clients and takes their cases to heart," Dr. Golden continued. "So when he loses, which is quite often, he takes it as a personal affront. He feels especially aggrieved by the case of his friend, Dr. Riggs, the former medical examiner, who lost his job in what Mr. Lassiter considers to be an unjust manner. As time goes on, his distrust of the system grows."

"I get that," the judge said. "But tell me how that affects Mr. Lassiter's capacity to practice law."

"Mr. Lassiter feels rage at the judicial system. Wherever he looks, he sees fraud, deception, and chicanery."

"What's crazy about that?" I chimed in.

"Quiet, Mr. Lassiter," the judge instructed. "No one says you're crazy. Or do they?"

"Crazy is a word that lacks meaning in my profession, Your Honor," Dr. Golden said. "I would venture to say, however, that Mr. Lassiter is delusional."

I stifled my desire to quack like a duck.

"Is he dangerous?" the judge asked.

"Certainly, he needs anger management counseling and rage control therapy. He should be closely monitored for signs of increased instability."

The judge chewed that over for a moment, then turned to Kim Coates. "What's the status of the lawsuit, *Farrell versus Lassiter*?"

"No progress to report, Your Honor," Kim said.

"Settlement negotiations?"

"None."

"Mr. Lassiter, the Court would look favorably on your settling the assault allegations by your former client."

I wanted to argue. I wanted to holler that threatening me with the loony bin was an improper way to force settlement. I wanted to say that, damn right, the justice system is run through with fraud, deception, and chicanery. That the Krippendorfs of this world are sleazy and corrupt and His Honor was a major tool.

But instead, I said, "Your Honor, I agree. Mr. Farrell can have everything in my bank account."

"Which is roughly what?"

"Roughly, overdrawn."

The judge narrowed his eyes and looked as if he wanted to throw his gavel at me. Instead, he put on his judicial voice and intoned, "Mr. Lassiter, I'm ordering that you report to Dr. Golden three times weekly for anger management treatment. Doctor, you'll report back to me in thirty days on Mr. Lassiter's progress or lack thereof. Ms. Coates, I'm ordering mediation of the underlying law-suit involving Mr. Farrell."

The judge turned back to me. "Finally, Mr. Lassiter, until next time, don't hit anybody, and in case you didn't hear me a moment ago, settle the damn lawsuit!"

TWENTY-FOUR

A Kiss Is Not Always a Kiss

Krippendorf offered his conference room for Silky's deposition. I declined.

Fine, he said. My office – such as it was – would work.

I declined that, too. I told him I wanted Silky to be comfortable, so let's do it at his house. Krippendorf agreed.

I wasn't even lying. I wanted Silky to be relaxed and confident. At first. By the time we finished, I wanted him confused and afraid.

Silky's house was a mini-manse on Star Island with about 300 feet of waterfront and dockage. A gazebo, cabanas, and entertainment area next to the infinity pool. Soaring spaces inside of marble, fine woods, vaulted ceilings, French doors, and – who can do without this in south Florida? – a magnificent stone fireplace. We set up for the depo in the library, a cool, dark wooded room with floor-to-ceiling shelves and thousands of record albums.

Silky wore, what else, a black silk shirt, unbuttoned, a heavy gold chain around his neck. Kim Coates sat next to him. The court stenographer typed away as I prodded.

"Isn't it true, Mr. Morton, that you own the original pressing of Charlie Christian's *Solo Flight?*"

"Objection," Kim sang out. "Irrelevant."

"Overruled," I said, as if I were the judge. "Kim, you know very well that objections need not be made at deposition to be preserved at trial, so I'll thank you for not interrupting my flow."

"There's a flow? I failed to detect that."

"Stick around and you might learn something."

"Jeez," Silky said, "you two got something going or what?"

"There's a question pending, Mr. Silky. Do you own the original pressing of Charlie Christian's *Solo Flight*?"

"The man practically invented the electric guitar, and I'm a collector."

"So the answer is yes."

"Hell, yes."

"What about Django Reinhardt's *Night and Day*?"

"Last cut before he died. Yeah, got that one."

"But you don't have Cadillac Johnson's *I'm Leaving You, Baby*."

"Wish I did, but it's impossible to find."

"Really? Your lawyers seemed to find a few and gobble them up."

"Is that a question?" Kim shot across the table.

"Yeah, for you. Do you think it's ethical to hide evidence?"

"You want my testimony, you better subpoena me."

"All I want to know," Silky said, eyes daring between the two of us, "is who dumped whom?"

"So you're denying you ever had in your possession a 45 rpm recording of Cadillac Johnson's *I'm Leaving You, Baby*?" I asked.

"Already said that."

"And you're also denying that you gave such a recording to Ms. Coates or anyone else at the Krippendorf law firm."

"Never gave nothing to nobody."

"And I resent the question's implication," Kim added.

I ignored her and plowed ahead. "Do you rent a safe deposit box?"

"Yeah, so what," Silky said.

"What do you keep in the box?"

"My will. Insurance policies. Some jewelry."

"Do you rent warehouse space?"

"I own a whole warehouse. Plus three homes, a condo, an R.V., and a customized bus. Search them all. I don't have that old man's song."

"Let's talk about the warehouse first," I said, as if I had all day.

"This is a waste of time, a fishing expedition," Kim said.

"But it's my pole and I paid for the license," I said. "Your warehouse, Mr. Silky. Where is it?"

Just then, my cell phone rang. I pretended to be surprised I hadn't turned it off. Feigned annoyance, too. "Yeah, what is it?" I said into the phone. "Really, Doc? Terrific! Call me later at home."

Kim and her client eyed me. I couldn't tell if their looks were suspicious or just intensely curious. I needed to toss some chum into the water and see how long until I got a bite. "We're done here," I said, cheerfully.

"Done?" Kim asked. "You've barely begun."

"Got everything I need."

"You've got nothing."

"You'd be surprised, Kim. I'll see you in court, Mr. Silky. Bring your checkbook."

I grabbed my briefcase and headed out of the library and down a corridor lined with framed platinum records. Before I reached the front door, Kim had caught up with me, just as I knew she would.

"What's going on, Jake?"

"Can't tell you."

"Your depo was a joke."

"You're not laughing"

In fact, she was scowling, and I hate to admit it, but that made her even more attractive in some perverse way.

"You can't stand it that I'm a better lawyer," she said.

"Not better. Nastier."

"If I were a man, you'd say I was 'powerful' and 'assertive.'"

"If you were a man, I'd punch you out."

She exhaled a long, exasperated sigh. Or maybe it was a hiss. Either way, she was pissed. "Why'd I ever waste a year on you?"

I gave her my crooked grin. "Because I let you take the top."

"You're ridiculous!"

"My headboard still has your scratch marks."

"And juvenile."

"I had to close the windows."

"And uncouth."

"Your screams scared the land crabs."

Without warning, Kim threw her arms around me, pulled me down to her level and kissed me. I could say that I shoved her away, but that would be a lie. I kissed her back. Long and slow. Sweet and soft, then harder and more urgently.

This time, her sigh was deep, and I swear a tear dripped from her closed eyes. I couldn't tell if she was pretending. But I knew I was.

TWENTY-FIVE

Night Games

The bedroom television was tuned to the Cartoon Network with the sound down. On the screen, an anvil dropped from a balloon and missed the Road Runner. But squashed Wile E. Coyote.

"Beep. Beep."

I was on my back in bed, Kim on top, straddling me. Grinding away. If I weren't enjoying myself so much, I'd say she was using me. Well, it's a messy job, but somebody has to do it.

Her head was tossing back and forth, her hair whipping across my face. It would have been a sexy move, except she resembled someone having an epileptic seizure. This went on for some time before she screamed something in Spanish, which surprised me, because she's not Hispanic, but that's the Miami cross-cultural influence for you.

I managed to time it so that we exploded more-or-less together. Then she collapsed onto my chest, her face pressed against my neck.

"Do you hate me?" she whispered.

"Intensely."

"I hate you more."

"I know."

She ran her lips along my neck and up my chin. Found my lips and kissed me.

I ran a hand up and down her spine.

"What are you doing?" she asked.

"Looking for a dorsal fin."

She kissed me again. "You know you're going to lose the case, right?"

"Nope. Don't know that."

"You have a very thick skull."

"Now, that I know."

"You have no evidence."

I gave her a crooked little smile. "Don't be too sure about that."

She studied me a long moment, wondering.

■■■

I fell asleep with Kim curled alongside me. When I awoke in the middle of the night, I felt as if I were sliding headfirst in a cloud of red dirt. It took a moment to clear the cobwebs. I'd been dreaming. One of those you clearly remember in the first seconds upon awakening.

A baseball game. I take a lead off first base. The pitcher is Krippendorf. If I had to guess, I'd say he's throwing spitters, but just now, he isn't looking at the batter. He's watching me take my lead. When he goes into his pickoff motion, I take off for second.

Krippendorf tosses the ball to the first baseman. It's Silky, who pivots and throws to the shortstop, covering second base. The shortstop is Bar investigator Grumley, who leaps high, but Silky's throw sails over his head into the outfield. I haul ass for third base. The left fielder, Judge Buckstrom, tosses a bullet to the third baseman, Judge Colton, but the ball gets past him. I chug home, running like hell. Colton's throw is on the money. The catcher, Kim, has her mask off and her makeup on. I slide head-first. She swipes at me, and misses!

The umpire, Doc Charlie Riggs, my only friend in the bunch, signals, "Safe!"

Awake now, I considered the dream a good omen. All my opponents dropped the ball. Unlike the play that gave rise to "Wrong

Way Lassiter," this was a good call. I had a distinct impression my luck was about to change.

After a few seconds, I realized I was alone in the bed. Another good omen. I knew Kim. Oh, how I knew her. There was very little chance she had gone home, and quite a strong chance that she was less than thirty feet away.

■■■

I could have stayed in bed. No matter what Kim did, I would have Silky under surveillance in the morning. But part of me just wanted to be certain, not about the case, but about her.

I padded out of the bedroom to the study, where a light was shining from under the closed door. No way I could open it without her seeing me. But in my mind, I knew what was happening inside. She was rifling my briefcase, looking for whatever scrap of evidence had made me so cocky. She wouldn't find a thing. But surely she would notice the flashing light on my answering machine. And knowing Kim, her insatiable desire to win at all costs would force her to look at the LCD window, which would show just how many calls were waiting.

I heard papers rustling, Kim saying something under her breath I couldn't entirely make out, but it might have been, "Shit, shit, double shit."

Then silence. Had she seen the flashing light? I heard the *click* of a button. Then the mechanical announcement that there were three new messages. The first one was a telemarketer's recorded voice asking if I wanted to consolidate my bills into one easy, monthly payment. *Click*, and the second message came on. Cece, my secretary, telling me about the next day's appointments, including one with a potential client, a fashion model, who wanted to sue a plastic surgeon for giving her C-cup breasts when she specifically asked for D-cups. Another *click*.

Doc Charlie Riggs's voice: "Great news, Jake! The P.I. found where Silky hid the record. We gotta get a court order before he moves it. I'll try you on your cell. Maybe you're still in depo. Jakey, my boy, we're gonna win!"

I wish I could have seen the look on Kim's face.

Then, pressing my ear to the door, I heard the faint pings of a phone being dialed. I didn't need to listen any longer. I knew who she was calling and what she would say.

TWENTY-SIX
Self Help

It was just after 9 a.m. when Doc Riggs called. I had been in my office since 8:15. Kim had declined breakfast and seemed cold and distant when she left. I figured by the end of the day, that would change to furious and vengeful.

"You were right, Jake," Charlie said.

"Right, how? Bank or warehouse?"

"Bank. Great Southern. Flagler Street just off Biscayne Boulevard. He just went inside."

"I'll be there in ten minutes. Twelve if the drawbridge is up."

"Okay, but what do I do if he comes out before you get here?"

"Just follow him. Don't be a tough guy."

■ ■ ■

Some days, everything works out just the way you plan. Not most days. Just some.

I found the last parking space along the median on Biscayne Boulevard and jogged to the bank. Charlie Riggs was sitting in his Dodge pick-up out front with the windows rolled down.

"He's still inside," Charlie said. "Now what?

"Now, I play tough guy."

It only took two more minutes. Silky headed out of the bank, nothing in his hands. No bag, no briefcase, no nothing. He wore a black silk Oakland Raiders jacket and black designer jeans. Guys

97

who aren't tough but want to be are always dressing in Raiders' silver and black.

Silky turned toward Biscayne Boulevard. I figure he was parked there, too. I cut him off just before he reached the corner.

"Yo, Silky."

"What the hell? Lassiter?" I couldn't see his eyes behind the aviator sunglasses, but I'd say there was a startled quality to his voice.

"Let's have it, Silky."

"Have what, shyster?"

"Give me the record. I have a court order."

Technically, that was an overstatement. I wished I had a court order, but I couldn't get one without prior notice to Krippendorf and that would have blown the whole scheme.

"Got no record, sucker."

"Then unzip your jacket and let me frisk you."

"Fuck you."

"The court order gives me the right to detain and search your person."

"Let me see that fucking order."

"As it so happens, I don't have it on me."

"Then fuck you, sideways."

I took a step toward him. "I'll have to use what the law calls self help."

"You touch me, I'll sue you for everything you've got."

"What I've got is an old car and a stack of bills."

I reached out to grab Silky by the collar of his Raiders' jacket. He swatted my hand away, turned and took off running, crossing the Boulevard against the light. I followed him, darting between cars, hearing curses and the bleat of horns. On the east side of the Boulevard, Silky passed the Torch of Friendship Monument and ran into Bayfront Park.

Silky seemed fast, but then he was wearing fancy Air Jordans, and I was chugging along in scuffed loafers.

I was never a speedster. In my playing days, I was too slow to be an outside linebacker, too small for the inside, and not athletic enough for either one. But I always had stamina. Now, even though I was falling behind Silky, I wasn't worried. My breaths were coming smoothly, and I could run all day.

I kept my head still, arms relaxed, pumping without flailing. Ahead of me, Silky's running style was, unlike his name, not smooth. Elbows flying, feet coming up high.

Silky was chugging down the steps of the empty outdoor amphitheater. I was twenty yards behind. I could smell the salt water of the nearby bay.

"You can't out-run me!" I shouted after him.

"Fuck you, shyster!"

I could hear the strain in his voice. A tortoise and hare deal.

Hell, I could have sung a song and kept running.

When Silky reached the stage, he turned right and headed south, deeper into the park. I had closed some of the distance, but he was still fifteen yards ahead. I could hear him gasping for air, which got me pumped. I picked up the pace and closed the gap just as we came to the children's playground. I pulled to within five feet as we passed the sculpture of a dolphin, manatee, and turtle playing under the lip of a breaking wave.

We were on sand now, so I sprinted a few more steps then dived at Silky, catching him behind the knees with my right shoulder. He shot forward, and I wrapped both arms around his legs, as if tackling a running back from behind.

He hit the sand with a *whompf* of air expelling from his lungs. I flipped him over and reached inside his Raiders' jacket. Felt something hard and slipped a 45 rpm record out of an interior pocket.

Of course, the label would say, *I'm Leaving You, Baby*. With Cadillac Johnson's name.

But it didn't. It said *Mack the Knife,* sung by Bobby Darin.

Holy shit!

"Where is it, Silky?"

He got to one knee, puffing hard. "Ain't got it."

"Bullshit! Where is it?"

"Gonna sue your ass, shyster. Don't care what you got. Gonna sue you your sorry ass just for the pure pleasure of it."

TWENTY-SEVEN

Human Factors

Ten minutes after my stalking, assaulting and battering M.C. Silky, I was in front of Great Southern Bank looking for Charlie Riggs. His pick-up truck was still there, but he wasn't.

I headed inside the lobby and found him shaking hands with a man in a gray suit.

"Then a court order it will be," Charlie said to the man, who walked back toward an interior office.

"I crapped out, Charlie."

"I know."

"How? What's going on here?"

"That was Mr. Stegmaier. Bank's head of security. He's going to get us the video tape that will show Silky coming out of the safe deposit area."

"What good will that do?"

"See that trash can by the pedestal desk." Charlie pointed toward the desk where customers fill out their deposit slips before approaching the tellers.

"Yeah, what about it?"

"I found this in the can." He reached into a pocket and pulled out a 45 rpm record. My breath caught in my throat as I turned it over.

At the top, the printing read, "Eddie Burns Records, New York, N.Y."

Underneath:

"I'm Leaving You, Baby. Cadillac Johnson."

A nice logo, too, the giant tail fins of a 1959 Cadillac El Dorado.

"Silky took it from his box and dumped it."

"You're amazing, Charlie. How did you know?"

"I didn't. Just thought there was a chance he'd never risk carrying the record out of the bank. When I walked inside, I noticed that trash can was in plain view of anyone leaving the safe deposit area. I've studied human factors a bit, you know. Even if Silky didn't intend to dump the record here when he entered the bank, seeing the can might have given him the idea. It certainly gave me the idea. But since I didn't see him put it there..."

"For evidentiary purposes, we need the security tape," I said, finishing his thought. "That'll tie up chain of custody."

"With a pretty bow."

I must not have looked joyful, because Charlie said, "What's wrong Jake? You're gonna win."

"Years."

"How's that?"

"It will take years of appeals. Like the George Harrison case with *My Sweet Lord.* Fifteen years! Cadillac doesn't have that kind of time."

"So what will you do?"

"Get Cadillac his money while it will do him some good."

"How?"

"Hit them hard and fast. And low."

TWENTY-EIGHT
Shove Your Rules

We were arranged around the polished mahogany table in Krippendorf's conference room.

A sullen Silky.

A glaring Kim.

A peaceful Cadillac.

Then there was the Kripster himself, shifting his prodigious bulk from one cheek to another in the high-backed cushioned chair at the head of the table.

And me. Jake Lassiter, 235 pounds of ex-football player, ex-night-school-law-student, ex-a-lot-of-things, confident and relaxed. I owned the moral high ground and was willing to come off the mountain and play in the gutter to keep it.

"Here's the story, Krip," I began. "Either we settle now, or I bring perjury charges against Silky and obstruction of justice against you and Kim."

"That's extortion!" Krippendorf protested.

"It's hardball. Care to play? That's what you said to me the last time we sat at this table."

If Krippendorf had been a cartoon character, smoke would have been streaming from his ears. "The Bar Rules are quite explicit," he said. "It's a violation to threaten criminal charges to settle a civil case."

"Hey, Krip. You can shove your Bar Rules where the sun don't shine."

"You son-of-a-bitch! I should have fired you sooner."

"You didn't fire me. I quit."

"Boys," Kim said, "please stop. Jake, what will it take?"

"Seven hundred fifty thousand." I felt Cadillac tugging at my sleeve. "Plus an apology."

"Forget it," Krippendorf said.

"I'm not done, Krip. The seven-fifty is from Silky. We'll take another two-hundred-fifty-thousand from you."

"You're dreaming. Fucking delusional."

"Count me in," Silky said.

"What!" Krippendorf shot a look at his client, mouth quivering. "I'll handle this, Silky."

"Like you handled everything else?"

"Just trust me, okay?"

"Give it up, man." Silky turned to me. "I just did what the lawyer man told me. And her, too." Looking at Kim now, whose glare never strayed from my face.

"Dammit, Silky!" Krippendorf said. "I said I'll handle it."

"No, you won't. You're fired."

Krippendorf recoiled as if slapped in the face.

Silky turned to Cadillac, shaking his head sadly. "I wanted to pay you, man. Apologize, too. But my rent-by-the-hour ho said you could never prove your case. Your lawyer was a loser."

Cadillac patted my arm. "Jake's got a good heart."

"And he runs like a brother," Silky said.

"Son-of-a-bitch," Krippendorf said.

"I'm sorry, man," Silky said. "I bit your music. Now, I'm gonna write you a check for three-quarters of a million bucks."

"Ain't accepting your apology," Cadillac said, then broke into a smile. "Not 'til the check clears."

"Which leaves your end, Krippendorf," I said. "Two-fifty."

"Not a chance."

"You've got ten seconds."

Finally, Kim spoke. "Jake, maybe there's a middle ground."

"No compromises. No deals, except mine. Five seconds."

Krippendorf looked away. I swear he was pouting.

"Three, two, one." I pulled my Motorola from my briefcase. "I'm calling the state attorney."

"Damn you, Lassiter!" Krippendorf's voice was thick with defeat.

"I'll draw up the documents." I didn't even try to keep the joy from my voice. "Cadillac, let's go get something to eat."

My client gripped my arm again with long, guitar-strumming fingers. "Dinner is on me, young man."

TWENTY-NINE
Success and Excellence

Twenty-four hours after Krippendorf folded like dirty laundry, I was jogging down Old Cutler Road, fighting the morning heat, swatting mosquitoes and gnats. Just as I crossed Casuarina Concourse, a black BMW convertible beeped its horn and pulled to a stop under a banyan tree, its nose blocking my path.

I recognized the car. And the driver. We'd played this scene before.

Kim Coates hopped out of the car, an envelope in her hand.

"You could have made an appointment," I said.

"Why should I? You're so predictable, I always know where you are." She tried to hand me the envelope. "Got something for you, Jake."

"If you're serving me papers again, I'm not here."

"Take it. There are two checks. One for you client, and one for you."

"On the other hand, I'm here." I opened the envelope. She hadn't been lying. Examining the first check, I read aloud. "Made payable to William Johnson a/k/a Cadillac Johnson. Six hundred sixty-six thousand, six hundred and sixty-six dollars."

"And sixty-six cents."

I looked at the second check. Made payable to me. Three hundred thirty-three thousand, three hundred, thirty-three dollars.

And thirty-three cents. By my calculations, they shortchanged us a penny, but I chose not to complain.

"Great, Kim. You need a receipt?"

"Only for Cadillac's check. Just endorse yours and give it back."

"Why would I do that?"

"Endorse it to James Farrell. As it turns out, he'll take a third of a million dollars to settle his claims against you."

"I never agreed to that," I said.

She proceeded, as usual, as if what I said didn't matter. "I have a release Farrell has pre-signed, in full satisfaction of his lawsuit. He'll also dismiss his Bar complaint."

"I said, I never agreed to settle."

"Or, I can tell Judge Buckstrom that you refused to settle, despite His Honor's direct admonition that you do so and despite the fact that you have the wherewithal to do so. Then we can proceed with Farrell's lawsuit and the Bar proceeding. Up to you, Jake."

Money has never been that important to me. Sure, that sounds strange coming from a lawyer. But I earned league minimum as a pro football player, and so far I'd never made any real dough practicing law. There's a disease in our culture where money is concerned. It's become the measuring rod of success. The bigger house, the fancier car, the juicier expense account. The acquisition of material things has become the hallmark of the shallow life. Which is why I seek "excellence," rather than "success."

Excellence measures the quality of work, not its financial payoff. I long for the cause that is just and the client who is deserving. Those two requirements alone often rule out a financial windfall. Too often in our justice system, money rides the back of the wrongdoer. The good are shuffled aside in the courtroom, just as they are on the streets.

But now I had achieved a just result for a deserving client. The only one to be shortchanged was me. Fine, there would be other cases.

"Do you have a pen?" I asked Kim.

She smiled as sweetly as she could, stifling the barracuda within. "Dinner tonight, Jake?"

"What? After the stunt I pulled on you?"

"The phony phone message? I admire your cleverness. How'd you know I'd go through your things?"

"Hell, you used to do that when we were on the same side of cases. You can't help yourself."

She was still smiling. What would be an insult to most people sounded like praise to her. "We have more in common that you think," she said.

"No way."

"C'mon, Jake. You break the rules to win."

"Only if my cause is just."

"Every cause is just if it's your cause. We'll work on that."

"There is no 'we.' No dinner, either. Not tonight. Not ever."

I took the envelope with Cadillac's check and jogged south, emerging from the shade of the banyan trees, feeling the luxuriant heat of the blazing sun.

THIRTY

Epilogue

Sherrell Johnson apologized for calling me names when I turned down the seventy-five thousand dollar offer.

Cadillac Johnson thanked me and said the retirement home he was moving into had a finely manicured croquet court if I wanted to come over for a game. He also invited me to a show he was putting on for the other residents, and I told him I'd be there.

Doc Charlie Riggs asked me to go fishing in the Glades, something that involved more drinking than casting, but I accepted that invitation, too.

My trusty secretary, Cece, finally hung my Road Runner and Wile E. Coyote posters on the walls of my garage office. She placed some more ads in the Beach Gazette, and the customers – I mean clients – started showing up. Just this morning, a nervous middle-aged lady came in with a tale of woe involving a second mortgage and an impending foreclosure sale of her house.

"You're my last hope, Mr. Lassiter," she said.

"Jake. Please call me Jake."

"Every lawyer in town has turned me down, Jake. They say my case is impossible."

"Then you've come to the right place."

She looked at me, her eyes wanting to believe I spoke the truth.

"If your cause is just," I said, "no case is impossible."

#

If you enjoyed "Last Chance Lassiter, please take a look at the rest of the award-winning series.

THE JAKE LASSITER SERIES

"Mystery writing at its very, very best." – Larry King, *USA TODAY*

TO SPEAK FOR THE DEAD: Linebacker-turned-lawyer Jake Lassiter begins to believe that his surgeon client is innocent of malpractice...but guilty of murder.

NIGHT VISION: After several women are killed by an Internet stalker, Jake is appointed a special prosecutor, and follows a trail of evidence from Miami to London and the very streets where Jack the Ripper once roamed.

FALSE DAWN: After his client confesses to a murder he didn't commit, Jake follows a bloody trail from Miami to Havana to discover the truth.

MORTAL SIN: Talk about conflicts of interest. Jake is sleeping with Gina Florio and defending her mob-connected husband in court.

RIPTIDE: Jake Lassiter chases a beautiful woman and stolen bonds from Miami to Maui.

FOOL ME TWICE: To clear his name in a murder investigation, Jake follows a trail of evidence that leads from Miami to buried treasure in the abandoned silver mines of Aspen, Colorado. (Ebook and new paperback edition.)

FLESH & BONES: Jake falls for his beautiful client even though he doubts her story. She claims to have recovered "repressed memories" of abuse...just before gunning down her father.

LASSITER: Jake retraces the steps of a model who went missing after his one-night stand with her 18 years earlier. (Ebook and new paperback edition.)

LAST CHANCE LASSITER: In this prequel novella, young Jake Lassiter has an impossible case: he represents Cadillac Johnson, an aging rhythm and blues musician who claims his greatest song was stolen by a top-of-the-charts hip-hop artist. (Ebook and new paperback edition).

STATE vs. LASSITER: This time, Jake is on the wrong side of the bar. He's charged with murder! The victim? His girlfriend and banker, Pamela Baylins, who was about to report him to the authorities for allegedly stealing from clients. (Ebook and new paperback edition).

Please also check out the short story "Solomon & Lord Sink or Swim" that immediately follows. Here are the full length novels in the series:

SOLOMON vs. LORD SERIES

(Nominated for the Edgar, Macavity, International Thriller, and James Thurber awards.)

"A cross between 'Moonlighting' and 'Night Court.' Courtroom drama has never been this much fun." – *FreshFiction.com*

SOLOMON vs. LORD: Trial lawyer Victoria Lord, who follows every rule, and Steve Solomon, who makes up his own, bicker and banter as they defend a beautiful young woman accused of killing her wealthy, older husband.

THE DEEP BLUE ALIBI: Solomon and Lord come together – and fly apart – defending Victoria's "Uncle Grif" on charges he killed a man with a speargun. It's a case set in the Florida Keys with side trips to coral reefs and a nudist colony where all is more –and less – than it seems.

KILL ALL THE LAWYERS: Just what did Steve Solomon do to infuriate ex-client and ex-con "Dr. Bill?" Did Solomon try to lose the case in which the TV shrink was charged in the death of a woman patient?

HABEAS PORPOISE: It starts with the kidnapping of a pair of trained dolphins and turns into a murder trial with Solomon and Lord on opposite sides after Victoria is appointed a special prosecutor, and fireworks follow!

Additionally, take a look at the author's
Stand-Alone Thrillers:

STAND-ALONE THRILLERS

IMPACT: A jetliner crashes in the Everglades. Is it negligence or terrorism? When the legal case gets to the Supreme Court, the defense has a unique strategy. Kill anyone, even a Supreme Court Justice, to win the case.

BALLISTIC: A nuclear missile, a band of terrorists, and only two people who can prevent Armageddon. A "loose nukes" thriller for the 21st century. (Also available in a new paperback edition.)

ILLEGAL: Down-and-out lawyer Jimmy (Royal) Payne tries to re-unite a Mexican boy with his missing mother and becomes enmeshed in the world of human trafficking and sex slavery.

PAYDIRT: Bobby Gallagher had it all and lost it. Now, assisted by his 12-year-old brainiac son, he tries to rig the Super Bowl, win a huge bet...and avoid getting killed in the process. (Also available in a new paperback edition.)

Visit the author's website at http://www.paul-levine.com for more information. While there, sign up for Paul Levine's newsletter and the chance to win free books, DVDs and other prizes.

BONUS MATERIAL:

"Solomon & Lord Sink or Swim"

"**R**emarkably fresh and original with characters you can't help loving and sparkling dialogue that echoes the Hepburn-Tracy screwball comedies. Hilarious, touching, and entertaining." *-Chicago Tribune* review of "Solomon vs. Lord"

There are four "Solomon vs. Lord" novels but only one short story, and here it is.

The sharpest lawyer to barely graduate from Key West School of Law, Steve Solomon is a beer and burger guy. Fresh from Yale, Victoria Lord is a Chardonnay and paté gal. The squabblers extraordinaire can't agree on "good morning," but somehow they're a winning team in court.

Steve plans a mysterious boat trip in the short story **"Solomon & Lord Sink or Swim."** He claims he's going fishing with Manuel Cruz, but Victoria isn't buying it. She knows that Cruz stole a bundle from Steve's favorite client. Victoria hops aboard to find out just what Steve has planned. The answer could get them both killed.

PAUL LEVINE
Author of *LASSITER*

SOLOMON & LORD
Sink or Swim

A Short Story Plus Bonus Material

SOLOMON & LORD SINK OR SWIM

"What aren't you telling me?" Victoria Lord demanded. *Jeez. Her grand jury tone.*

"Nothing to tell," Steve Solomon said. "I'm going deep-sea fishing."

"You? The guy who got seasick in a paddle boat at Disney World."

"That boat was defective. I'm gonna sue." Steve hauled an Igloo cooler onto the kitchen counter. "You may not know it, but I come from a long line of anglers."

"A long line of liars, you mean."

The partners of Solomon & Lord, Attorneys-at-Law, stood in the kitchen of Steve's bungalow on Kumquat Avenue in Coconut Grove. The place was a square stucco pillbox the color of a rotting avocado, but it had withstood hurricanes, termites, and countless keg parties.

Unshaven and hair mussed, wearing cargo shorts and a t-shirt, Steve looked like a beach bum. Lips glossed and cheekbones highlighted, wearing a glen plaid suit with an ivory silk blouse, Victoria looked sexy, smart, and successful.

"C'mon, Steve. What are you really up to?" Her voice drizzled with suspicion like mango glaze over sautéed snapper.

Steve wanted to tell his lover and law partner the truth. Or at least, the partial truth. But he knew how Ms. Propriety would react:

117

"You can't do that. It's unethical."

And if he told her the truth, the whole truth, and nothing but the truth? *"You'll be disbarred! Jailed. Maybe even killed."*

No, he'd have to fly solo. Or swim solo, as the case may be.

Steve pulled two six packs of Heineken out of the refrigerator and tossed them into the cooler. "Okay, it's really a business meeting."

Victoria cocked her head and pursed her lips in cross-exam mode. "Which is it, Pinocchio? Fishing or business? Were you lying then or are you lying now?"

For a tall, lanky blonde with a dazzling smile, she could fire accusations the way Dan Marino once threw the football.

"I'm going fishing with Manuel Cruz."

"What! I thought you were going to sue him."

"Which is what makes it business. Cruz wants to make an offer before we file suit. I suggested we go fishing, keep it relaxed. He loved the idea and invited me on his boat."

So far, Steve hadn't told an outright fib and it was almost 8 a.m. Not quite a personal best, but still, he was proud of himself.

For the last five years, Manuel Cruz worked as controller of Toraño Chevrolet in Hialeah where he managed to steal three million dollars before anyone noticed. Teresa Toraño, a Cuban *exilado* in her seventies, was nearly bankrupt, and Steve was determined to get her money back, but it wouldn't be easy. All the computer records had been erased, leaving no electronic trail. Cruz had no visible assets other than his sportfishing boat. The guy didn't even own a house. And the juiciest piece of evidence – Cruz fled Cuba years ago after embezzling money from a government food program – wasn't even admissible.

"Just you and Cruz, alone at sea." she said. "Sounds dangerous."

" I'm not afraid of him."

"It's not you I'm worried about."

■■■

Victoria punched the RECORD button on her pocket Dictaphone. "Memo to the Torano file. Make certain our malpractice premiums are paid."

"You and your damned Dictaphone," Steve complained. "Drives me nuts."

"Why?"

"I don't know. It's so..."

"Organized?"

"Anal."

Victoria pulled her Mini-Cooper into the Matheson Hammock marina, swerving to avoid a land-crab, *clip-clopping* across the asphalt. The sun was already baking the pavement, the air sponge-thick with humidity. Just above a stand of sea lavender trees, a pair of turkey buzzards flew surveillance.

Victoria sneaked a look at Steve as he hauled the cooler out of the car's tiny trunk. Dark, unruly hair, a slight, sly grin as if he were one joke ahead of the rest of the world. The deep brown eyes, usually filled with mischief, were hidden behind dark Ray Bans.

Dammit, why won't he level with me?

Why did he always take the serpentine path instead of the expressway? Why did he always treat laws and rules, cases and precedents as mere suggestions?

Because he has more fun making it up as he goes along.

Steve drove her crazy with his courtroom antics and his high-wire ethics. If he believed in a client, there was nothing he wouldn't do to win. Which was exactly what frightened her now.

Just what would Steve do for Teresa Torano?

They headed toward the dock, the morning sun beating down so ferociously Victoria felt her blouse sticking to her shoulder blades. The only sounds were the groans of boats in their moorings and the *caws* of gulls overhead. The air smelled of the marshy hammock, salt and iodine and fermenting seaweed. The fronds of thatch palms hung limp in the still air.

"Gimme a kiss. I gotta go," Steve said, as they stepped onto the concrete dock. In front of them were expensive toys, gleaming white in the morning sun. Rows of powerful sportfishermen, large as houses. Dozens of sleek sailing craft, ketches and sloops and schooners.

"Sure, Mr. Romance." She kissed him lightly on the lips. Something seemed off-kilter, but what? And what was that pressing against her through his shorts?

Hadn't last night been enough? Twice before SportsCenter, once after Letterman.

She sneaked a hand into his pocket and came out with a pair of handcuffs. "What's this, the latest in fishing tackle?"

"Ah. Well. Er..." Gasping like a beached grouper. "You know that store, *Only Sexy Things?*" He grabbed the handcuffs and slipped them back into his pocket. "Thought I'd spice up the bedroom."

"Stick to cinnamon incense. Last chance, lover boy. What's going on?"

"You're fucking late, *hombre!*" Manuel Cruz yelled from the fly bridge of a power boat tied up at the dock. He was a muscular man in his late thirties, wearing canvas shorts and a white shirt with epaulets. A Marlins' cap was pulled low over his eyes, and his sunglasses hung on a chain.

The boat was a sportfisherman in the sixty-foot range, all polished teak and gleaming chrome. A fly bridge, a glass enclosed salon, and a pair of fighting chairs in the cockpit for serious deep-sea fishing. The name on the stern read: "*Wet Dream.*"

Men, Victoria thought. Men were so one-dimensional.

"*Buenos días*, Ms. Lord."

She gave him a nod and a tight smile.

"Let's go, Solomon," Cruz urged. "Fish are hungry."

Steve hoisted the cooler onto the deck. "Toss the lines for us, hon?"

She leveled a gaze at him. "Sure, *hon*."

Victoria untied the bow line from its cleat and tossed it aboard. She moved quickly to the stern, untied the line, propped a hand on a piling crusted with bird dung, and leapt aboard.

"Vic! Whadaya think you're you doing?"

"Going fishing."

"Get back on the dock."

She smiled and pointed toward the increasing body of water that separated them from land.

"You're not dressed for fishing," Steve told her.

"I'm dressed for your bail hearing." She kicked off her velvet-toed pumps and peeled off her panty hose, distracting Steve with her muscular calves, honed on the tennis courts of La Gorce Country Club. "Now, what's with the handcuffs?"

Steve lowered his voice so she could barely hear him above the roaring diesels. "You remember Solomon's Law number one?"

Oh, that. Steve's personal code for rule breaking.

"How could I forget? 'If the law doesn't work...work the law.'"

"In the matter of Manuel Cruz, the law isn't working."

■■■

"What's that?" Cruz asked, eying the cooler on the deck.

"Brought beer and bait," Steve said.

"What for? I got a case of *La Tropical* and a hundred pounds of shiners and wiggles."

All three of them stood on the fly bridge. Twin diesels throbbing, the *Wet Dream* cruised down Hawk Channel inside the barrier reefs. The water was green felt, smooth as a billiard table, the boat riding on a plane at thirty knots.

Cruz ran a hand over the polished teak steering wheel. "I come to this country with nothing but the clothes on my back and look at me now."

"Very impressive," Steve said, thinking it would be even more impressive if Cruz hadn't stolen the money to buy the damn boat.

Cruz winked at Victoria, his smile more of a leer. "You two want to fool around, I got clean sheets in the master stateroom."

"Sounds lovely," Victoria cooed. "Want to fool around, Steve?" Her smile was as sweet as fresh-squeezed *guarapo*, but Steve caught the sarcastic tone.

"Maybe after we catch something," he said, pointedly.

"Heads and A/C work, faucets don't," Cruz said. "Water tank's fouled."

Steve studied the man, standing legs spread at the wheel, a macho pose. A green tattoo of a scorpion crawled up one ankle. On the other ankle, in a leather sheaf, was a foot-long Marine combat knife. It looked like the weapon Sylvester Stallone used in those "Rambo" movies. Out here, it could be used to cut lines or clean fish.

Or gut a lawyer planning to do him harm.

■ ■ ■

They had just passed Sombrero Light when Cruz said, "So here's my offer, *hombre*. The Toraño bitch gives me a release with a promise never to sue. And vice versa. I won't sue her ass."

"I don't like the way you talk about my client," Steve said.

"Tough shit. I don't like Fidel Castro, but what am I gonna do about it?"

"Your offer stinks like week-old snapper."

"You sue me, what do you get? A piece of paper you can wipe your ass with. I got nothing in my own name, including the boat."

Steve looked right and left to get his bearings. Off to port, in the direction of the reef, he spotted the fins of two sharks heading toward strands of yellow sargasso weed, home to countless fish. Red coral just below the surface cast a rusty glow on the shallow water. To the starboard was the archipelago of the Florida Keys.

From here, the island chain was strung out like an emerald necklace. "Let Vic take the wheel a minute," Steve said. "I want you to see something."

Cruz allowed as how even a woman lawyer could keep a boat on 180 degrees, due south, and followed Steve down the ladder to the cockpit. Just off the stern, the props dug at the water like a plow digging at a field. Steve opened the cooler, reached underneath the ice and pulled out a two foot-long greenish-blue fish, frozen solid. A horse-eyed jack.

"Great bait, huh?" Steve held the fish by its tail and let it swing free. It had a fine heft, like a small sledgehammer.

"Already told you. I got shiners and wiggles."

"Then I better use this for something else." Steve swung the frozen fish at Cruz' head. The man stutter-stepped sideways and the blow glanced off his shoulder and sideswiped an ear. Steve swung again, and Cruz ducked, the fish flying free and shattering the glass door of the salon. Cruz reached for his knife in the ankle sheath and Steve barreled into him, knocking them both to the deck.

On the fly bridge, Victoria screamed. "Stop! Both of you!"

The two men rolled over each other, scraping elbows and knees on the planked deck. Cruz was heavier, and his breath smelled of tobacco. Steve was wiry and quicker, but ended up underneath when they skidded to a stop. Cruz grabbed Steve's t-shirt at the neck and slammed his head into the deck. Once, twice, three times. *Thwomp, thwomp, thwomp.*

Steve balled a fist and landed a short right that caught Cruz squarely on the Adam's apple. The man gagged, clutched his throat, and fell backward. Steve squirmed out from under, but Cruz tripped him. Steve tumbled into the gunwale, smacking his head, sparks flashing behind his eyes. He had the sensation of being dragged across a hard floor. On his back, he opened his eyes and saw something glistening in the sun.

The knife blade!

Cruz was on his knees, knife in hand. "*Pendejo!* I oughta make chum out of you."

"No!" Victoria's voice, closer than it should have been.

Steve heard the *clunk*, saw Cruz topple over, felt him bounce off his own chest. Straddling both of them was Victoria, a three-foot steel tarpon gaff in her right hand. "Omigod," she said. "I didn't kill him, did I?"

"Not unless a dead man grunts and farts at the same time," Steve said, listening to sounds coming from both ends of the semi-conscious man.

He shoved Cruz off and stood up, wrapping his arms around Victoria, who was trembling. "You were terrific, Vic. We work great together."

"Really? What did you do?"

"Come on. Help me get him up the ladder." Steve pulled the handcuffs from his pocket. "I want him on the bridge."

"What now? What insanity now?"

"Relax Vic. In a few hours, Cruz will be dying to give back Teresa's money."

■■■

Steve had played fast and loose with the rules before, Victoria thought, but nothing like this.

This is scary. And in the eyes of the law, she was dirty, too.

This could mean trading the couture outfits and Italian foot-wear for orange jumpsuits and shower shoes.

With one wrist handcuffed to the rail at the rear of the bridge, Cruz had been berating Steve for the past twenty minutes. "Know what, Solomon? She hits harder than you do."

"Mr. Cruz," Victoria said, "if you begin to feel dizzy or nau-seous, let me know. Head trauma can be very dangerous."

"What about *my* head?" Steve demanded.

"It's impervious to trauma. Or reason."

The *Wet Dream* was planing across the tops of small whitecaps when Steve said: "Take the wheel, Vic. Keep it on two-zero-two."

"*Please*," she said, irritated.

"What?"

"'Keep it on two-zero-two, *please*.'"

"A captain doesn't say 'please.'"

"Maybe not Captain Bligh." Victoria slid behind the wheel, thinking maybe she'd hit the wrong man with the gaff. She still didn't know where they were headed, and Steve's behavior was becoming increasingly bizarre. He had the beginning of a lump on his head, and blood trickled from his skinned elbows and knees.

"Kidnaping," Cruz said. "Assault. Boat theft. You two are gonna be busy little shysters."

"Shut up," Steve said. "Under the law of the sea, I'm master of this craft."

"What law? You stole my fucking boat."

■■■

Once past Key West, they entered the Florida Straits, the water growing deeper, the color turning from light green to aquamarine to cobalt blue. No reefs here, and a five-foot chop slapped at the hull of the boat. The wavecaps sparkled, as if studded with diamonds in the late afternoon sun.

"Gonna tell you a story, Cruz," Steve said, "and when I'm done, you're gonna cry and beg forgiveness and give back all the money you stole.'"

"Yeah, right."

"Story starts forty-some years ago in Havana. A beautiful lady named Teresa Toraño lost her husband who was brave enough to oppose Fidel Castro."

"Tough shit," Cruz said. "Happened to a lot of people."

"Teresa came to Miami with nothing. Worked minimum wage, mopped floors in a car dealership, ended up owning Toraño Chevrolet."

" My *papi* always told me hard work pays off," Cruz said, smirking. "Too bad he never got out of the cane fields."

"A few years ago, she hires a new controller. A fellow *exilado*. This guy's got a fancy computer system that will revolutionize their books. It also lets him steal three million bucks before anybody knows what hit them. Now, the banks have pulled Teresa's line of credit, and she could go under."

"I'm not crying, Solomon."

"Not done yet. See, this lady is damn important to me. If it hadn't been for Teresa giving me work my first year out of school, I'd have gone broke."

"Lo único que logró la dama fue posponer lo inevitable," Cruz said. "She only postponed the inevitable."

Victoria knew there was more to it than just a financial relationship. Teresa had virtually adopted Steve and his nephew Bobby, and the Solomon Boys loved her in return. After Victoria entered the picture, she was added to the extended Toraño family. Now, each year at Christmas, they all gathered at Teresa's estate in Coral Gables for her homemade *crema de vie,* an anise drink so rich it made eggnog seem like diet soda. All of which meant that Steve would do anything for Teresa. One of Steve's self-proclaimed laws expressed the principle:

"I won't break the law, breach legal ethics, or risk jail time...unless it's for someone I love."

Now that Victoria thought about it, the question wasn't: *Just what would Steve do for Teresa Toraño?* It was: *What* wouldn't *he do?*

"That sleazy accountant," Steve said. "In Cuba, he kept the books for the student worker program, the students who cut sugar cane. Ran the whole food services division. But he had a nasty habit of cutting the pineapple juice with water and selling the meat off the back of trucks. The kids went hungry and he got fat. When the authorities found out, he stole a boat and got the hell out of the worker's paradise."

"Old news, *hombre*."

"Vic, still on two-zero-two?" Steve asked.

"I know how to read a compass," she said, sharply.

"Where you taking me?" Cruz demanded.

"Jeez, how'd you ever get from Havana to Key West?" Steve said.

"Everybody in Havana knows the heading to the States. You want Key West, you keep it at twenty-two degrees."

"A bit east of due north. So what's two-zero-two?"

"A little west of due south."

"Keep going, Cruz. I think you're catching the drift, no pun intended."

Steve waited a moment for the bulb to pop on. When it didn't, he continued, "Two hundred two minus twenty-two is one hundred eighty. What happens when you make a hundred eighty degree turn, philosophically or geographically speaking?"

"Fuck!" Cruz jerked the handcuff so hard the rail shuddered. "We're going to Havana!"

"Bingo. We're repatriating you."

"You crazy? Cuban patrol boats will sink us. You remember that tugboat. *Trece de Marzo*. Forty people dead."

"The *Marzo* was trying to *leave* the island. We're coming in, and we're bringing a fugitive to justice. They should give us a reward, or at least a bottle of Club Havana rum."

"They'll kill me."

"Not without a trial. A speedy trial. Of course, if you tell us where you've stashed Teresa's money, we'll turn this tub around."

"Dammit, Steve," Victoria said. "We have to talk."

■ ■ ■

Steve put the boat on auto – two hundred two degrees – and took Victoria down to the salon.

"You could get us killed," she said. "Or jailed. Right now, the best case scenario would be disbarment."

"That's why I didn't want you along."

Steve walked to the galley sink and turned on the faucet, intending to rinse the dried blood from a scraped elbow. The plumbing rattled and thumped, but nothing came out. He opened the ice maker. Empty, too.

"Cruz is a lousy host," Steve said.

"Are you listening to me? Let's go back to Miami. I'll see if we can talk Cruz out of filing charges."

They both heard the sound, but it took a second to identify it. A scream from the bridge. "Sol-o-mon!"

Followed a second later by machine gun fire.

■ ■ ■

Steve and Victoria ran back up the ladder to the bridge. Cruz was tugging against the rail, his wrist bleeding where the handcuff sawed into his skin. Three hundred yards off their starboard, a Cuban patrol boat fired a short burst from a machine gun mounted on its bow. Dead ahead, the silhouette of the Cuban island rose from the sea, misty in the late afternoon light.

"Warning shots," Steve said. "Everybody relax."

Steve eased back on the throttles, tooted the horn, and waved both arms at the approaching boat. "C'mon Cruz. It's now or never. When they pull alongside, I'm handing you over."

"Do what you got to do, asshole."

"Steve, turn the boat around," Victoria ordered. "Now!"

The patrol boat slowed. Two men in uniform at the machine gun, a third man holding a bullhorn.

"I'm not fucking with you, Cruz," Steve said. "You've got thirty seconds. Where's Teresa's money?"

"*Chingate!*" Cruz snarled.

"*Senores del barco de pesca!*" The tinny sound of the bullhorn carried across the water.

"Last chance," Steve said.

"*Se han adentrado en las aguas territoriales de la República de Cuba.*"

"Steve, we're in Cuban waters," Victoria said.

"I know. I passed Spanish 101."

"*Den la vuelta y salgan inmediatamente de aquí, o los vamos a abordar.*"

"They're going to board us if we don't turn around," she said.

"I kind of figured that out, too." Steve turned to Cruz. "Absolutely, positively last chance, pal. I'm handing you over."

"I'm betting you don't," Cruz said.

The patrol boat was fifty yards away. One of the men in uniform pointed an AK-47 their way.

"Steve...?" Victoria's voice was a plea.

This wasn't the way he'd planned it. By this time, Cruz should have been spouting numbers and accounts from banks in the Caymans or Switzerland or the Isle of Man. But the bastard was toughing it out. Calling Steve's bluff.

Is that what it is? An empty threat.

Steve wanted to hand Cruz over, wanted him to rot in a Cuban prison.

But dammit, I'm a lawyer, not a vigilante.

He wished he could turn his conscience on and off with the flick of a switch. He wished he could end a man's life with cold calculations and no remorse. But the rats that would gnaw at Cruz at *Isla de Pinos* would visit the house on Kumquat Avenue in Steve's nightmares.

"Take the wheel, Vic." Filled with self-loathing, wishing he could be someone he was not. "Twenty-two degrees. Key West."

"Say 'please,'" Cruz laughed, mocking him.

■■■

Just before midnight, the lights of Key West off the port, the *Wet Dream* cruised north through Hawk Channel, headed toward Miami. The sky was clear and sparkled with stars. The wind whipped across the bridge, bringing a night chill. Victoria slipped into her glen-plaid jacket. Hair messed, clothes rumpled, emotionally drained, she was trying to figure out how to salvage the situation.

I came aboard to save Steve from himself and I'm doing a lousy job.

Steve stood at the wheel, draining a *La Tropical beer*, maybe listening, maybe not, as Cruz berated him.

"You fucking loser," Cruz said. "Every minute I'm tied up is gonna cost you." Cruz rubbed his arm where the cuff was biting into his wrist. "I got nerve damage. Gonna add that to my lawsuit. When this is over, you'll wish the Cubans had taken *you* prisoner."

"Steve, I need a moment with you," Victoria said.

Steve put the boat on auto – Cruz complaining that it was a damn reckless way to cruise at night – then headed down the ladder, joining Victoria in the salon.

"You can't keep him locked up," she said.

"I need more time."

"For what?"

"To think." He walked to the galley sink and turned the faucet, intending to toss cold water on his face. Same rattle, same thump. "Damn, I forgot. Cruz put all that money into his boat and still can't get the water to work."

"What?"

"A fancy boat like this and you can't wash your hands."

"No. What you said before. 'Cruz put all that money into his boat.'"

"It's just a figure of speech."

"Think about it, Steve. He doesn't own a house. He leases a car. No brokerage accounts, no bank accounts. Everything he has, he puts into his boat. If he ever has to leave town quickly…"

"Like he left Cuba," Steve said, picking up the beat. "With nothing but the clothes on his back."

"This time it would be different because..."

"The money's here! On the boat."

In sync now, she thought.

A man and a woman running stride for stride.

"Vic, why don't you go back up to the bridge and make sure we don't crash into any cruise ships?"

"And what are you doing?"

"I'm gonna fix the plumbing."

■■■

Steve opened the hatch in the salon floor and climbed down a ladder to the engine compartment, wincing at the noise from the twin diesels. He found the black water tank first, tucked up under the bow. Sewage and waste water. Nothing unusual about it, and Cruz wouldn't want to dirty his hands with that, anyway. Then Steve found the freshwater tank, a custom job built into one of the bulkheads. Made of fiberglass, it looked capable of holding 500 gallons or more. The boat had desalinization equipment, so why did Cruz need such a big tank?

A big tank that wasn't working.

Steve grabbed a flashlight mounted on a pole and took a closer look. He peered into an inspection port and could see the tank was three quarters full. On top of the tank was a metal plate with a built-in handle. He turned the plate counter-clockwise and removed it. Then he aimed the flashlight into the opening.

Water. Well, what did you expect?

He grabbed a mop that was attached by velcro to a stringer and poked the handle into the tank. The end of the handle *clanked* off the walls.

Clank. Clank. Clank. Thud.

Thud? What the hell?

Steve pushed the mop handle around the bottom of the tank as if he were stirring a giant vat of *paella*. It snagged on something soft. He worked the handle under the object and lifted.

Something as long as a man's body but much thinner.

Thin enough to fit into the opening of the custom-built tank. The object was a transparent, plasticized pouch, and when the end peeked out of the opening, Steve saw Ben Franklin's tight-lipped face. A hundred dollar bill. Stacked on others. Dozens of stacks. As he pulled the pouch out of the tank, he saw even more. Hundreds of stacks, thousands of bills.

■ ■ ■

Damn heavy, Steve thought, lugging the pouch up the ladder from the engine compartment. Then he dragged the load out the salon door and into the cockpit. "Now you've done it," Cruz sounded almost mournful. He stood on the bridge, aiming a double-barrel shotgun at Steve. The rail where he had been cuffed hung loose. "I didn't want this. But it's your own damn fault."

"I'm sorry, Steve," Victoria said. "When I came up here, he'd gotten out."

"Not your fault," Steve said. He dragged the pouch to the starboard gunwale.

"Stop right there!" Cruz ordered. "Step away from the money."

"Nope. Don't think so."

Cruz pumped the shotgun, an unmistakable *click-clack* that Steve felt in the pit of his stomach. "I'll blow your head off."

"And leave blood and bone and tissue embedded in the planking? Nah. You may kill us, but you won't do it on your boat." Steve hoisted the pouch onto the rail.

"If I can't take this to Teresa, I'm sure as hell not gonna let you have it. Your treasure, pal, is strictly Sierra Madre.'"

The shotgun blast roared over Steve's head, and he flinched. The pouch balanced on the rail, halfway between the deck and the deep blue sea.

"Put the money down, asshole."

"Okay, okay." Steve shoved the pouch over the rail and it splashed into the water. "It's down."

"Asshole!" Cruz grabbed both throttles, slowed the boat, and swung her around. He turned a spotlight on the water.

Nothing but a black sea and foamy whitecaps.

He swung the spotlight left and right. Still nothing, until...the beam picked up the pouch floating with the current. Cruz eased the boat close to the pouch at idle speed, slipped the engine out of gear, then dashed down the ladder. Grabbing a tarpon gaff, he moved quickly to the gunwale. Shotgun in one hand, gaff in the other, he motioned toward Steve. "Back up. All the way to the chair."

"Do what he says, Steve," Victoria called from the bridge.

"Only because you said so." Steve moved toward one of the fighting chairs.

Cruz leaned over the side and snagged the pouch with the gaff. He struggled to lift it with one arm, still aiming the shotgun at Steve.

Suddenly, the boat shot forward, and Cruz tumbled into the water, the shotgun blasting into space as it fell onto the deck. On the bridge, Victoria had one hand on the throttles, the other on the wheel.

"*Cono!*" Cruz shouted from the darkness.

"Do sharks feed at night?" Steve leaned over the side. " Or should I just drop some wiggles on your head and find out?"

"Get me out of here!" His voice more fearful than demanding.

"Nah."

"*No me jodas!*"

"I'm not fucking with you. Just don't feel like giving you a lift."

Victoria raced down the ladder and joined Steve in the cockpit. "Testing, testing," she said, punching a button on her pocket Dictaphone.

"What are you doing?" Steve said.

"Mr. Cruz," Victoria called out. "We'll bring you on board once you answer a few questions."

Cruz was splashing just off the starboard side. "What fucking questions!"

"Do you admit stealing three million dollars from Teresa Toraño?" Victoria said.

■ ■ ■

Pink slivers of sky lit up the horizon and seabirds squawked overhead as Steve steered the boat into the channel at Matheson Hammock. He had one hand on the wheel and one draped on Victoria's shoulder. A shivering Cruz, his arms and legs bound with quarter-inch line, was laced into a fighting chair in the cockpit. His taped confession would be in the hands of the State Attorney by noon. The pouch of money lay at his feet, taunting him.

"What are you thinking about?" Victoria asked.

"I was just imagining the look on Teresa's face when we give her the money."

"She'll be delighted. But it was never about the money, Steve."

"Whadaya mean?"

"When you were a baby lawyer, Teresa believed in you and nobody else did. You needed to prove to her that she was right. And maybe you needed to prove it to yourself, too."

Steve shrugged. "If you say so."

She wrapped both arms around his neck. "But remember this, Steve. You never have to prove anything to me." They kissed, at first softly, and then deeper and slower. The kiss lasted a long time, and when they each opened their eyes, the sun was peeking above the horizon in the eastern sky.

Their bodies pressed together, Victoria felt something digging into her hip. "Are you carrying another pair of handcuffs?"

"Nope."

"Then what...?" She jammed a hand into one of his pocket. "Oh. That."

Steve smiled. "Like I said, no cuffs."

"That's okay, sailor." She brushed her lips against his cheek. "You won't need them."

#

If you enjoyed the short story, please try any
of the full length novels in the series.

SOLOMON vs. LORD SERIES

(Nominated for the Edgar, Macavity, International Thriller, and James Thurber awards.)

"A cross between 'Moonlighting' and 'Night Court.' Courtroom drama has never been this much fun." – *FreshFiction.com*

SOLOMON vs. LORD: Trial lawyer Victoria Lord, who follows every rule, and Steve Solomon, who makes up his own, bicker and banter as they defend a beautiful young woman accused of killing her wealthy, older husband.

THE DEEP BLUE ALIBI: Solomon and Lord come together – and fly apart – defending Victoria's "Uncle Grif" on charges he killed a man with a speargun. It's a case set in the Florida Keys with side trips to coral reefs and a nudist colony where all is more –and less – than it seems.

KILL ALL THE LAWYERS: Just what did Steve Solomon do to infuriate ex-client and ex-con "Dr. Bill?" Did Solomon try to lose the case in which the TV shrink was charged in the death of a woman patient?

HABEAS PORPOISE: It starts with the kidnapping of a pair of trained dolphins and turns into a murder trial with Solomon and Lord on opposite sides after Victoria is appointed a special prosecutor, and fireworks follow!

ABOUT THE AUTHOR

The author of 16 novels, Paul Levine won the John D. MacDonald fiction award and was nominated for the Edgar, Macavity, International Thriller, and James Thurber prizes. A former trial lawyer, he also wrote more than 20 episodes of the CBS military drama "JAG" and co-created the Supreme Court drama "First Monday" starring James Garner and Joe Mantegna. The critically acclaimed international bestseller "To Speak for the Dead" was his first novel. He is also the author of the "Solomon vs. Lord" series and the thrillers "Illegal," "Impact," "Ballistic," and "Paydirt." You can sign up for the author's free newsletter and be eligible for signed books, DVDs and more at http.//www.paul levine.com

Made in the USA
Las Vegas, NV
24 January 2022

42186735R00090